Never Say No to a Killer

CLIFTON ADAMS

Black Gat Books • Eureka California

NEVER SAY NO TO A KILLER

Published by Black Gat Books
A division of Stark House Press
1315 H Street
Eureka, CA 95501, USA
griffinskye3@sbcglobal.net
www.starkhousepress.com

NEVER SAY NO TO A KILLER
Originally published by Ace Books, New York, and
copyright © 1956 by A. A. Wyn, Inc., as by Jonathan
Gant. This edition published under the author's real
name, Clifton Adams.

ISBN-13: 978-1-944520-36-6

Book design by Mark Shepard, SHEPGRAPHICS.COM

First Stark House Press Edition: November 2017

FIRST EDITION

CHAPTER ONE

The rock was about the size of a man's head. A beautiful rock, about twenty pounds of it, and somehow I had to get over to it. The minute I saw it I knew that rock was just the thing I needed. This is going to take some doing, I thought, but I have to get my hands on that rock.

Gorgan yelled, "Get the lead out, Surratt! This ain't no goddamn picnic!"

Gorgan was one of the prison guards, a red-faced, hairy-armed anthropoid, sadist by instinct, moron by breeding. His lips curled in a grin and he lifted his Winchester 30-30 and pointed it straight at my chest. There was nothing in the world he would like better than an excuse to kill me. He had had his eye on me for a long time.

You sonofabitch, I thought, if you knew what was good for you, you would pull that trigger right now, because five minutes from now it's going to be too late!

But not now. Right now I was going to be the model prisoner, I was going to dig into that stinking, smoking asphalt and I was going to let Gorgan enjoy himself. In the meantime I *had* to get to that rock.

There were fourteen of us out there, twelve prisoners and two guards. We were right out in the middle of God's nowhere. Somebody had got the bright idea that the prison needed an air strip, a place where the State dignitaries could set their planes down. So that's what we were doing out there, building the air strip.

We were about three miles from the prison, four miles from the main highway, and about six miles from the prison town of Beaker. Hard against the prison, to the south, there was a big oil refinery, so we had to get on the other side of the refinery to build the air strip. The only reason we were left out there with just two guards was we were trustees. Pounding scorching asphalt ten hours a day, under a hundred degree sun, was supposed to be a privilege.

Well, I was going to kick their privilege right in the face!

But first I had to get to that rock. It was about twenty feet from us, over by the edge of the asphalt strip, so I began working my big wooden smoother over in that direction. Gorgan, feeling that he had got a hook in me, was reluctant to let it go. He moved over to the edge of the strip, that 30-30 still aimed at my heart.

"Get the lead out, Surratt! This ain't no goddamn picnic!"

One dump truck had emptied its load near the end of the strip and was now headed back toward Beaker. Another truck was just beginning to tilt its bed. This would be the last truck we'd see for at least an hour—which was fine, just the way I wanted it. But I had to work fast now. I had to get things started before that truck driver finished unloading.

I lifted my head for just an instant, just long enough to get the complete picture in my mind. The other prisoners were slightly ahead of me, with their heavy smoothers, tampers, rakes, wading ankle deep in that steaming black slush. The other guard, a kid of about twenty-three, was over by the water keg having himself a smoke. I heard the dump truck's winch growl, the bed tilted sharply and the black mass poured into a smoking pile on the ground.

The time had come.

I looked at that rock; I looked at it harder than I ever looked at anything in my life. I could almost feel that 30-30 of Gorgan's and knew that he still had it pointed at me. There was absolutely no telling what an idiot like Gorgan would do at a time like this. This was the most dangerous moment. The rest of it was planned—right at this moment, John Venci was waiting for me in Beaker. Five years I had worked on this, and it was perfect—all but this particular instant. I had to drop my smoother; I had to bend down and pick up that rock; and I had to do it while looking right into the muzzle of that Winchester.

I prayed that Gorgan's neolithic brain was working. If his brain worked, I was all right. If he simply reacted, like an animal, then I was sunk. That trigger finger would twitch and I would never know what hit me.

It was a calculated risk. I had to take it.

I kept staring at that rock. I had to slip the clutch before I started. I had to somehow make contact with that apelike mentality of Gorgan's, and the best way to do it was through curiosity. I stared at that rock as though it were the great-grandfather of all the rocks in the world. I grunted, as though in amazement. Then I dropped the smoother. I bent down and took the rocks in my hands.

"Surratt! Goddamn you, I told you once ...!"

I held the rock tenderly. I held it as though it were pure gold. I had gotten away with it! I had aroused the ape's curiosity!

"Mr. Gorgan," I said, never taking my eyes off that rock, "this is the damnedest thing I ever saw!"

"You bastard!" he snarled, "put that thing down and pick up that smoother! Or maybe you want to know what a 30-30 slug in the guts feels like!"

I had him hooked. I could feel it. He was looking at that rock and not paying so much attention to his rifle.

"Look at this, Mr. Gorgan!" I said. "What do you make of this?"

He was hooked, all right! He forgot for a moment that he hated me. The ape thought he had found something. Something valuable, maybe, or anyway something very curious. He moved toward me, his flat, red face jutting forward.

His forehead wrinkled perplexedly, almost as though he were in pain. "What the hell! It's just a rock!"

"But look at this, Mr. Gorgan!" I pointed to a place on the rock—a place where there was nothing. Gorgan came closer. He saw nothing.

At that instant I think Gorgan knew he was as good as dead. I could see it in those animal-like little eyes.

That was when I brought the rock up with all the strength I had in my two arms. It cracked the point of Gorgan's chin and I heard his jawbone snap under the impact.

He didn't make a sound. He dropped his rifle and started to fall.

It was very fast and clean. I felt the strength of ten men as I watched him sprawl out with his face in the hot asphalt. "Good-by, Gorgan," I thought. Then I picked up his rifle and shot him.

The other guard, the twenty-three-year-old kid, was still over by the water keg. He looked as though the sky had fallen. I started to yell and tell him to leave his rifle alone and he wouldn't get hurt, but I saw in an instant that it would only be a waste of breath.

He was a born hero, that kid. You could read it in every outraged line of his face. He made a dive for his rifle which was leaning against the water keg, but by that time I had made up my mind about heroes. He fired a quick one, a wild one, the slug missing me by a full fifty feet, and then I got the center of his chest in my sights and pulled the trigger. He jerked back, as though he had been hit in the gut with a hammer, and then he fell sprawling, a dead hero.

The truck driver was next. He was a smart boy and he certainly was no hero. I yelled for him to get out of the cab and he got out, fast, his hands in the air.

"Just stay there, just the way you are," I said, and he nodded eagerly.

The other prisoners hadn't done a thing. They stood there like dumb cattle, too exhausted to make a move or a sound. The hell with them, I thought, and jogged over to the water keg and picked up the dead hero's rifle.

I called to the truck driver: "Start getting out of your clothes, and be quick about it!"

I skinned out of my dungaree prison jacket and trousers and got into the truck driver's blue work shirt and khaki pants. I felt like a new man.

"Do you have a watch?" I said.

He held out his arm, offering me his wrist watch.

"Mister," he said tightly, "you want the watch, take it."

I laughed at him. "That's considerate of you, but all I want is the time."

It was eleven-fifty, which was just about perfect. Noon is the dullest time of day—comes twelve o'clock and everybody knocks off for lunch, even cops. Even prison officials and truck drivers. That was how I knew that no more trucks would be coming to the air strip until the noon hour was over. If anybody wanted to spread the alarm, they would have to walk clear to the refinery, or to the highway which would give me plenty of time to make my contact with John Venci in Beaker.

"Don't get any cute ideas," I said, "about slamming this truck into gear and getting away from me."

His face was very pale. "Mister, do I look like a fool?"

I laughed. "No, you don't. I'd say you're a very wise man."

CHAPTER TWO

It went like clockwork. It couldn't have been more than twelve-fifteen when I parked the truck in an alley behind a Beaker lumber yard.

I had been in the town before, but towns change over a period of five years, and it took a few minutes to get my bearings. To me the town was as exciting as Manhattan. Five years! I got out of the truck and stood there breathing in the air, smelling the smells. Who would ever believe that a man could gorge himself on thin, pure air!

I could do it. I drank it in like some fabulous gourmet tasting a really great wine for the first time, better than anything I had ever tasted before. It was freedom.

I was almost drunk with the realization that I was actually free. I walked away from the truck, and the dirty sidewalks of that dirty little town couldn't have felt better if they had been strewn with Persian carpets.

I noticed a clock in a jewelry store window, and that brought me back to the business at hand. I had almost finished with my part in the escape, and now it was up to John Venci. I didn't let myself consider the possibility that Venci wouldn't hold up his end of the bargain. He just had to be there, that's all there was to it. If he wasn't, then it was the end of Roy Surratt, and that was one thing I didn't let myself think about.

I quickened my pace and reached the end of Main Street where there was a service station—that was the first check point. Up ahead was a car. It was a new one and it was in the right place. I felt like laughing when I saw that car. It was all I could do to keep from running.

Then the roof fell in. I got even with the car and saw that it wasn't Venci at all, it was a woman. She just sat there, looking straight ahead. I felt as though somebody had opened my veins and drained out all my strength.

Where the hell was Venci! This was the place. I knew it was. But where the hell was he! I walked past the car and the woman didn't make a move. I could feel panic's cold hand on the back of my neck.

I walked to the end of the block and looked back. The car and the woman were still there, and there was still no sign of John Venci.

Get a good hold, Surratt, I told myself, because it's a long way down if you fall! I might as well face it; Venci wasn't there, and he wasn't going to come. Maybe something had gone wrong at his end, or maybe he had simply decided that the risk was too great and had forgotten it. From now on I was on my own, and the odds were a million to one that I would never get out of Beaker alive.

Venci I would take care of later, if I lived that long. Right now there was no time for anger. There was no time for anything except trying to think of a way to get out of this death trap before the alarm sounded. I thought of the freight yards, hitch hiking, stealing a car, and gave them all up immediately. Then I turned and headed back toward town, and I looked at that parked car again.

I knew what I was going to do.

I was going to take that car, woman and all. If the going got rough, she would be my hostage.

I walked around to the driver's side of the car, jerked the door open and said, "Lady, if you enjoy living, just don't make a sound,"

I ducked my head inside. She looked at me for just a moment, then said, "You must be Roy Surratt."

I stared at her. "What?"

"I said you must be Roy Surratt. I'm Dorris."

I just looked at her.

"Dorris Venci," she said shortly. "John Venci is my husband. Now will you please get in the back seat; there are some clothes back there for you."

She was no raving beauty, but there was something about her that got you. I said, "Mrs. Venci, you just about gave me heart failure. What happened to John?"

She frowned impatiently. "Later. Do you want to get in the back seat or don't you?"

I opened the door and got in the back seat. Laid out beside me was a complete set of street clothes. "Change as quickly as possible," she said. "I'll let you know if anyone comes."

I started peeling down without a second invitation. "While I'm doing this," I said, "will you tell me what this is all about?"

"John is sick," she said flatly, "so I came in his place."

"What's wrong with him?"

She said nothing.

"All right, I was just asking," I said. "Where do we go from here?"

"That depends on what we hear on the radio. If it seems safe we'll go all the way to the city where—where we have made plans for you. If anything comes up I'll have to drop you off with some people I know."

I looked out the back window; the street was deserted. I said, "I'm a little out of practice with ties. Have you got a mirror?"

She got one out of her bag and held it up. What I saw was a sun-browned man of thirty-four, dark hair, regular features. He was no matinee idol, but he wasn't bad looking, either.

"Do you want me to drive?" I asked.

"Yes, that might be better."

I got out of the back seat and into the front, under the wheel. She said, "Was there much trouble?"

"No trouble at all," I said. "It went like clockwork. But we'd better get out of here pretty quick because in about thirty minutes hell's going to break loose."

Dorris Venci said, "It doesn't seem possible that an escape could be brought off with no trouble at all."

"Well, there were two guards. I had to kill them."

She looked at me. "That's nice," she said. "I'm glad there wasn't any trouble."

"I tell you it's all right, Mrs. Venci. It will be at least thirty minutes before anybody finds out about it. There's nobody out there but a few prisoners and a truck driver. By the time the news gets out, we'll be a long way from Beaker. Everything was planned and everything went just the way I wanted it."

She said, "Do you know how to find State Highway 61?"

"Sure."

"All right, if you are through congratulating yourself, perhaps we can get started."

I laughed. "Whatever you say, Mrs. Venci."

We got out of town and on the highway with no trouble at all. I kept looking at myself in the rear view mirror; I couldn't get enough of looking at myself in a tie and clean white shirt. I had killed Gorgan; I had made my escape; and now I was behind the wheel of a sleek new automobile.

I didn't know the radio was on until it suddenly blared out: "GREENLEAF CALLING CAR 202!"

That is all there was to it.

"What was that?" I said.

"The radio is tuned to the State Highway Patrol frequency," Dorris Venci said. "Car 202 is beyond our range; that's why we couldn't hear the reply."

"But we can hear the Patrol headquarters. Is that right?"

"Yes. When news of your escape reaches the prison officials they will notify the Patrol"

"And the Patrol will notify us."

"If we are still within range."

That short wave radio made a great impression on me. Why, with a thing like this working for him, a man could get away with murder! They'd never catch him. Then I thought: What are you thinking about, Surratt? You are getting away with murder, right this minute!

I looked at Dorris Venci, really looked at her, for the first time. Until now I had been much too busy with myself to pay attention to anything else, but now that it looked like clear sailing I turned my attention to John Venci's wife.

My first impression of her had been pretty accurate. She was good looking, but certainly no raving beauty. She was a pretty good sized girl, maybe five-six, with a rather prominent bone structure. She had a good figure, too—maybe not one to stop traffic, but plenty good enough. All a man could reasonably ask for in a woman.

Her eyes were what stopped you. I decided. They were large and dark and very clear. Looking into her eyes was like looking into a pair of beautifully polished Zeiss lenses; they gave you a feeling of great depth and emptiness.

She could have been thirty-five or twenty-five—sometimes it is hard to tell about big girls. The longer I looked at her the more beautiful she seemed to get, but I put that down to my being locked away from women for five years.

I hadn't even known that Venci had a wife, but there were a lot of things about Venci that I didn't know. Our acquaintance, although it had been very satisfactory, had been a brief one. An obscure gambling law had landed him in the State penitentiary for a short stretch, and for a few days we had been cell mates. We hadn't dwelt on personalities at all—only ideas; so it wasn't surprising that he had failed to mention Dorris.

"What time is it?" I asked.

She looked at her watch. "A quarter of one."

"It won't be long now. I'd like to see that warden's face when he gets the news. What did I tell you? Nobody but a handful of convicts know I've escaped."

The radio made a liar out of me. We were moving out of line-of-sight broadcast range, but not so far out that we couldn't hear Patrol headquarters when the news broke. Both of us listened intently for several minutes as my description was given: a description of the truck driver's clothes that I was supposed to be wearing, a description of the truck I was supposed to be driving.

I laughed. "What a shock they would get if they could see their escaped convict now, decked out in an oxford gray suit, driving a new Lincoln, a beautiful woman beside him."

"That's enough of that," she said. "We have a long way

to go before you are safe."

"All right, but could you tell me just where we are going?"

"To Lake City, if there are no complications. You will be safe there for a while."

"Lake City suits me fine. By the way, it occurs to me that I haven't thanked you for everything you've done."

"Don't bother," she said, looking straight ahead. "This isn't a free ride. You'll be expected to earn your passage when we get to Lake City."

I would earn my passage, all right. I had known that from the first; it didn't bother me—John Venci's work was my kind of work, and we'd get along.

That started me thinking about Venci, and the way we had arranged this escape almost a year ago. It had been a beautiful set-up, as absolutely perfect as a circle. We had started with a basic truth which held that the actual prison break was the least important detail of a successful escape. With a little care, any moron could crash out of prison— he could stay on his good behavior, become a trustee and simply walk away, if that's all there was to it.

But there was a lot more to it than that. Those first few hours, those first two or three hours after the initial crash-out—they were the hours that killed you. You had to have help, that was the main thing, and without it you were beat before you started. "The initial break," Venci had told me, "will be up to you. Nine months and I'll be out of this place; I'll be in a position to help you, but I'm not going to try anything as crude as smuggling you a gun, is that clear?"

"Perfectly."

"Nine months you'll have to think about it, make it good."

"I could do it tomorrow. I could crash out of this rock pile and make it as far as Beaker before they knew what hit them."

"Nevertheless, you will wait the nine months if you really mean business, if you have the brains I think you have."

He was completely humorless, John Venci—or I had thought so at the time. He was small, lean, extremely intense, and he had a brain that was as immaculate and keen as a scalpel. When John Venci took a liking to a man it made all the difference in the world; you were suddenly somebody to be reckoned with, you amounted to something. No con dared cross you after the word got around that John Venci had taken a liking to you—it was the best thing that could happen, and it had happened to me. On the other hand, the worst thing that could happen to a man was to get Venci down on you, and the cons knew that too.

Almost from the first we had hit it off, which may sound strange. John Venci was old enough to be my father. He was the master of his calling, which was crime. His organization had a thousand brains and two thousand arms— arms that could reach anywhere, grab anything. "I don't get it," I had said once, "a man like you, a gambling rap's nothing. Why did you stand still for it? Why did you allow yourself to be put away for a stretch, even a short one?"

Paper-thin lids had dropped over his intense eyes, and he had smiled with no more expression than a razor gash in a piece of leather. "Suppose," he said, "that a very religious man feels the overpowering need for meditation, for reconsecration of his flagging spirit, where does he go?" I said, "A monastery, I suppose." "Exactly," he had answered. "Well, I came to prison."

That was John Venci. A purist, a theorist, a perfectionist in crime. John Venci had intelligence and imagination— and I think he was slightly mad.

I wanted to talk about escape, and Venci would deliver

a lecture on abstract theories of vengeance. I had believed in them. Our personal philosophies gave us common ground from the very beginning. No longer was I a nobody. No longer was I just another punk who had blundered on his first bank job.

"This is amazing!" Venci had said.

I said, "I fail to see anything amazing in the fact that I have learned to read and am capable of thought."

"Nevertheless, it is amazing! Materialism makes an intriguing theory, but how many people have the guts to believe it, actually believe in it, right to the bottoms of their bleak little souls? How many have you known?"

"Not many, I guess."

"Do you know why? It knocks their crutches from under them, that's why. They simply don't have what it takes to purge themselves of their fantastic little guilts...."

Then he had stopped, his eyes alive, and he had interrupted himself calmly: "I have in mind a certain ... project. A rather audacious project, I might say, even for me. It will take a good deal of thought ... as well as action. Strange, until now I had not envisioned another actor in this—particular little drama of mine ..." He had studied me bleakly, in sober concentration. "Yes," he had said finally, "I think I could use you, Roy Surratt."

"I can't do you much good if I stay in this cell the rest of my life."

"No.... Do you have a specific plan in mind?"

"Yes. You'll be out of here in nine months. In nine months I'll be ready. I'll be the best prisoner they ever saw; I'll be the darling of every screw in the yard; I'll endear myself to every goddamn contract guard that comes within ass-kissing distance of me. I'll make myself Warden's pet even if it makes me vomit. In short, I'll be a trustee, and the initial crash will be a cinch. After the break I'll make it into Beaker under my own steam, and I'll somehow arrange it so that the alarm doesn't get out immediately. Forty-five minutes or an hour, I'll need that much start at least, and I'll get it."

He said nothing, so I went on. "All right, we assume, then, that I can make the break and reach Beaker before a general alarm goes out. The town of Beaker, that's where I must have help. I must have a getaway car, and not a hot one, either. I must have a complete outfit of clothes, some money, some escape routes planned in case the unforeseeable should happen. That's the way it has to be if I'm to get out of that town alive."

"Yes.... It can be arranged."

"Fine. Now for the details for your end of it. First, a contact point. And a time for the contact. Noon is the best time, so we'll make it between twelve noon and one o'clock. Now the place. I used to know the town pretty well—let's see, at the north end of Main Street there is a big service station, just before you get to the railroad tracks. That's a good place, easy to spot. Now west of that service station there is a quiet residential street, as I remember, which should be all right. The second block to the right of that station, midway in the second block, between twelve noon and one o'clock, is that all right for the time and place of contact?"

"You make it sound pretty simple."

"It *will* be simple. I'll keep it as simple as it humanly possible. After I work on this thing for nine months it will be perfect—all I want to know is do you go for it?"

Only a moment's hesitation, then positively: "I go for it. I'll see to it myself, but only for one day a week, over a three month span from the day they release me."

"That's fair enough, make it Friday. Friday's the best day, it's always the most hectic, and if there is a shortage of guards it will be on Friday, just before the week end."

For one long moment he had said nothing. At last he murmured, "Yes ... Yes, it sounds all right." Then, with no warning at all, he stepped forward and hit me in the mouth with his fist.

The suddenness of the attack stunned me. I reeled back and crashed against the bars of the cell. "Goddamnit," John Venci hissed under his breath, "fight!"

Then I got it. In case of an assisted escape, the cops always suspected the escapee's friends, and John Venci was merely striking off such a possibility. The entire cell block seemed to know the instant the first blow was struck. At the top of his lungs, John Venci yelled, "You sonofabitch!" Then he grabbed up a stool and hurled it at me, and the place burst into bedlam as every con in the block began rattling bars and yelling. All right! I thought. All right, there's no sense doing a thing half way! We might as well make it look good!

My mouth was pouring blood, and I'd caught one of Venci's shoe heels under my left eye. He kept digging in as though his very life was at stake, cursing and yelling like a crazy man, as savage as a lion. But it was no match. He was tough, all right, and vicious, but I had weight and youth on my side, and every time I knocked him crashing against the bars I thought: Jesus, I hope those goddamn guards break it up before I kill him!

So that was John Venci, as I knew him. He played it to the hilt, and by his rules only the winner ever walked away. After the brawl, after the guards finally got tired clubbing us, after their legs wearied from kicking us, they finally dragged us off to the hole.

I don't know what John Venci thought about during his stay in solitary, probably it didn't bother him at all.

What I thought about was that escape. I nursed my two splintered ribs and tried to breathe as lightly as possible, and thought of that dazzling day nine months in the future when I would crash out of this hell hole for good. And when I did, somebody was going to pay for those two splintered ribs.

Still, the thing that fascinated me most through those endless days of darkness was the fact that I never doubted John Venci. When the time came, he would be there, and I never doubted it for a second. I understood that it was not going to be a free ride, and that I would have to "earn" my passage, as Dorris Venci had put it.

That was fine with me; I had never cared for free rides anyway.

CHAPTER THREE

We hit town about nine o'clock that night, Dorris Venci and I, and quite a town it was, too. It was like a fairyland, all that color, the dancing lights, garish show windows, the buildings.

I was completely delighted. "This is the most wonderful thing I ever saw," I said.

Dorris Venci said, "Turn left at the next corner. I'll tell you where to go from there."

I was afraid she was going to take me away from the lights. I felt like a child who had been allowed to watch a carousel for a moment and then jerked away. "Where are we going?" I said.

"Stop here," Dorris said.

"Here on the corner?"

"Yes. The Tower Hotel is just across the street. Go to the desk and tell the clerk you are William O'Connor from Dallas; he has your reservation."

"This is going to be a little rich for me at first, but I hope to get used to it. What do you do while William O'-Connor checks in?"

"Take the car around to the hotel garage. Stay in your apartment; I'll want to talk to you later."

"All right, but shouldn't I have some luggage or something. It's going to look pretty fishy walking into a hotel like that without any luggage."

"That's been taken care of," she said. "The luggage is already in your apartment."

She thought of everything. Well, almost everything. I got out of the car, and then turned back again. "I hate to bring this up," I said, "but could you let me have a dollar?"

She frowned. "Why?"

"Unless hotels have changed a lot in five years, the boy who shows me to my room is going to expect more than handshakes and fond wishes."

It wasn't good for a laugh, or even a smile. She got a five dollar bill out of her bag and handed it to me. I hadn't thought much about it until now, but she was in a pretty sour mood and had been ever since I had known her. I headed for the lobby.

"Mr. O'Connor ..." The desk clerk frowned, thumbing through his reservation file. "Oh yes, Mr. *O'Connor*, here we are." He smiled, suddenly glad to see me. He motioned to a bellhop and said, "821 for Mr. O'Connor. Your luggage is already in your apartment, sir; hope you enjoy your stay."

"I'm sure I will." I smiled and tried to keep my dirty hands and grimy fingernails hidden in my pockets.

The so-called apartment was nothing special, but it was certainly better than a prison cell. I gave the bellhop the five and he took it as though it were a debt long overdue.

"Would there be anything else, sir?"

"No, thank you; that's all I can afford."

I got the fish eye for an instant, just before he slipped out the door. Well, I thought, it has been a busy day. It has been the most wonderful day of my life. I owed John Venci plenty, for what he had done for me this day, and I didn't mean to forget it. He could have anything he wanted out of Roy Surratt, all he had to do was ask.

I opened the bedroom closet and there were two leather

suitcases with the initials W. O'C. stamped in gold letters near the handles. I opened them up and there was more haberdashery.

I was standing at the window looking out at the city and all those exciting, dazzling lights, when there was a knock at the door. It was Dorris Venci.

"I was just looking at the city," I said. "You have no idea how beautiful it is to me. Look at the way those lights shimmer, they never stand still. A painter would have a hell of a time getting a thing like that on canvas."

Dorris Venci frowned. "What are you talking about?"

I laughed, "Nothing, I guess. It's just that there are a lot of sights and smells and sounds and experiences that I haven't been exposed to for a long time. I'll get over it."

"I hope it's soon. Is the apartment all right?"

"The apartment is fine, but I'm not sure I understand all you're doing for me. Don't get me wrong, I appreciate all this and expect to pay for it, but it seems like a lot of trouble to go to when all I expected was a lift out of Beaker." Dorris looked at me, then moved across the room and sat on the edge of an uncomfortable sofa. "By the way," I said, "when do I get to see your husband? He's not too sick to talk, is he?"

Without a flick of an eyelash, she said, "My husband is dead."

I wasn't sure that I had heard her correctly. "What did you say?"

"My husband is dead. He was murdered a week ago."

This news stunned me. After all that had happened, after all that he had done for me, I simply couldn't believe that John Venci was dead. But it was no joke—a person didn't joke while looking at you the way Dorris Venci was looking at me. John Venci *was* dead. It was a fact that I had to get used to.

"I think I'll sit down," I said. Now I knew why she had that soured-on-the-world look.

I took a chair on the other side of the small coffee table and looked at Dorris Venci. "Your husband was quite a man, Mrs. Venci," I said. "I didn't know him long enough to know whether I liked him or not, but I did admire him. There are very few people in this world who share that particular distinction."

"Just how well did you know my husband, Mr. Surratt?"

"Not very well, as I told you. He was in my cell three days and then they separated us. Oh, I knew who he was, all right. He was the boss of Lake City."

She smiled, completely without humor. "Would you tell me what you and my husband talked about in prison?"

"A lot of things: both of us had a great admiration for realists, the only real philosophers of modern times. Do you think philosophy a strange subject for a prison discussion? Well, it isn't. A man has to think in prison—work and think—that's about all he has time for. The bad thing about it is that there are so very few people in prisons who are capable of thinking. We spoke about the freedom of the individual."

"I see. The freedom of the individual to do as he pleases."

"The freedom of the individual to do as he pleases, providing he has the necessary strength."

"Yes, there is a difference, isn't there. Tell me, Mr. Surratt, if you had all the money you could ever want, how would you live out your later years?"

"Probably I would retire and concentrate on killing all the people I didn't like."

"That," she said, "is what my husband did."

I sat there for a full thirty seconds without making a move.

She was completely serious. Her face was set and her eyes were as cold as gun steel. This, I thought, is the wildest thing I ever heard of in my life ... but I believed it. So now I knew why John Venci had bothered to spring me—he had foreseen the possibility of his own murder and had wanted a man on his side that he could trust.

But I was too late. Venci was dead.

After a moment she said, "Mr. Surratt, did it ever occur to you, while you were in prison, that my husband might not keep his part of the escape bargain?"

"Never. After that fight of ours I never saw him again, but I never stopped believing. You know why? Because your husband needed me as much as I needed him. For what reason, I didn't know at the time; I just knew we needed each other. He wanted a man he could trust right up to the brink of death, and that was me, because we had the same kind of brains.

"I understand some things now. You just said that your husband had set out to dispose of his enemies—that can be dangerous business, very dangerous, with the kind of enemies John Venci had. He was afraid his enemies would try to kill him before he killed them, and he wanted me around to see that it didn't happen."

Mrs. Venci said, "You are wrong again, Mr. Surratt. John Venci was afraid of no one or no thing." She stood up, suddenly. "I'm not sure that I need your help, after all, Mr. Surratt."

I believe she would have walked out of the room if I hadn't crossed in front of her. "All right," I said, "I'm wrong. But how about setting me right?"

"I'm not sure I can trust you."

"If you can't trust me, whom can you trust?"

Yes, who could she trust? Not many people would be capable or willing to pick up John Venci's fight, against John Venci's enemies. "Very well," she said, after a moment's hesitation. "I'll think about it. I'll contact you to-morrow."

"Just a minute," I said. "Do you happen to know a beauty operator you can trust?" Her eyebrows came up just a little. "I want my hairline changed," I said, "and my hair bleached. I also want a pair of horn-rimmed glasses with plain lenses."

"That can be arranged," she said, "if it proves necessary." She went out.

We hadn't mentioned money, but I was thinking money all the time. I was thinking of all that money John Venci had made. It was Dorris's money now. And she wasn't a bad looking woman, either. Oh, no, I thought, she's not going to get rid of me now!

CHAPTER FOUR

The first thing I did the next morning was take a shower. A shower six times a day, I thought, every damn day until I get the stench of that prison out of my body and soul.

At last I got out of the shower and walked naked and dripping into the sitting room and called room service. "I'd like to order breakfast," I said. "A large pot of coffee and a New York cut steak, sautéed in butter."

There was one thing that Dorris Venci had forgotten when she outfitted me and that was a razor. I called the bell captain and told him to hustle me a razor, and then I went back to the bathroom and showered all over again.

In the light of this new day, I could accept the death of my benefactor with calmness. John Venci was dead and there was nothing I could do about it, so I accepted it. The situation wasn't exactly as I had planned it, but I had to make the best of it. And that was exactly what I intended to do.

I had finished the steak and eggs and was working on the orange juice and coffee when the telephone rang. It was Dorris.

"You're moving," she said.

"Is that so?"

"This is the address. 2209 North Hampton. Come to apartment 7."

"Is that all I need to know?"

"Yes." She hung up.

It was about ten o'clock when I got to the North Hampton address. It was a run-of-the-mill apartment building and not very fancy, certainly not as fancy as the Tower Hotel. I found apartment 7 on the first floor and knocked. There was no answer. I tried the door and it was unlocked, so I walked in.

It was a dark, dank-smelling place; sitting room, bedroom and bath—the same setup I'd had at the hotel. I raised the shades to let in some light, then took an armchair to wait. Maybe five minutes went by, then the door opened and Dorris came in.

"You're prompt," she said. "That's something."

"What's the idea of moving me to a place like this? It smells of mice and empty bean cans."

"Is it worse than the place you had yesterday?"

It was almost impossible to believe that I had been a convict only yesterday, that I had been wading ankle-deep in stinking asphalt, taking all kinds of crap from sadistic idiots like the late Mr. Gorgan. This place wasn't so bad after all.

Dorris had a large bundle in one arm and a newspaper under the other. She handed me the newspaper and went into the kitchen with the other stuff.

"You made the front page," she said.

"So I see."

"You're on the radio, too."

"I'll bet you anything in the world they're already calling me the Mad Dog killer. And Gorgan will be made out a hero. But he'll be a dead one; you can bet your sweet life on that!"

Dorris stepped into the kitchen doorway. "You say that as though you enjoyed killing him."

"I enjoyed killing Gorgan. It was about the most exhilarating experience of my life just watching the sonofabitch die."

She stood there for a minute, then went back in the kitchen. She was busy doing something, but I was too satisfied and full of good food to get up and see what it was. I read part of the escape story, but it was the usual crap.

Dorris said, "Remember what I told you when I brought you to Lake City, that you would have to earn your passage?"

"I remember."

She came into the room this time and stood there in front of me, looking at me. "The time has come," she said. "I want you to kill a man."

I wasn't in the least surprised. I had known all along that the man who pulled the trigger on John Venci was going to get killed, and probably by me. It was in Dorris Venci's eyes every time she mentioned her husband's name.

"I'm in debt to you," I said. "I was in debt to your husband, too. A lot of things have been said about Roy Surratt, but nobody ever accused him of welshing on a debt. Whom do you want killed?"

She stared at me for a full half minute. "Until I let you in my car yesterday," she said quietly, "my husband was the only completely evil man I ever knew. But you're just like him; you're enough like him to be the son he never had."

This jarred me a bit, since I had been going under the assumption that Dorris Venci had loved her husband. But I was beginning to learn that she was the kind of woman who said and did some pretty erratic things, things that you had to take in stride.

"I'll take that as a compliment," I said. "By my rules it would be a great honor being John Venci's son. But let's get something straight, just for the record. This person you want killed, he's the one who murdered your husband, or had it done, isn't he? That being the case, you must have loved your husband very much, in spite of this thing that obsessed him, this thing you call 'evil'. Or maybe because of it. You don't have to answer, because it is written all over you; you loved him. What I want to know is why do you look down your nose at me if I'm so much like the husband you loved?"

She just stared at me with those Zeiss-lens eyes of hers. I didn't like being stared at like that; it was about time to take Dorris Venci down a peg or two.

"You know," I said, "I've got a funny feeling about you, Mrs. Venci. You brought up the subject of evil just a minute ago, and still you were in love with a man like John Venci. Now a situation like that makes for some interesting theorizing. Apparently you have a perfectly normal and conventional loathing for evil, but a look at the record will show that you are obviously attracted by it, too. Wouldn't you say this is an interesting contradiction?"

I smiled, enjoying myself. She wasn't so damn snooty now, and there was a difference in the way she stared at me.

"Interesting," I said, "still these contradictions are encountered every day. Sane-mad, pro-anti, they're all separated by the thinnest thread. One kind of fanaticism can be exchanged for another."

She stood there rigid and icy. "Roy Surratt!" she sneered. "Murderer, thief, blasphemer. You're a fine one to talk about fanaticism."

"Tell me something, just one more thing. I'd like to know why a woman who loathes evil would marry a man like John Venci."

I stared into the empty depth of those empty eyes and knew that she was frightened. She almost frightened me, the way she looked.

I had started the thing as a gag because she had made me sore. There I was offering to kill a man, just for her, because she wanted him killed. I was going to do it, and what did she do? She had stood there looking down her nose at me, looking at me as though I'd been something the dog had dragged in on her clean carpet, and that made me burn!

That was when I had started probing. We'll see about this superior business, I thought. I'll stick pins in her, and keep sticking pins in her until I hit a nerve, and then we'll just open her up and see what makes this bitch tick. I was getting pretty tired of people looking down their noses at me.

Now she just stood there, staring.

What the hell have I got on my hands? I thought. Christ, she gave me the willies, standing there like a piece of ice statuary, those eyes of hers fixed on me.

You'd better figure it out, I thought, and pretty fast too, because she looks like she's about ready to blow up in your face. Oh, she looked cool enough, she looked icy, but a bomb looks cool too until you move up closer and hear the timing mechanism ticking away the seconds, and then you know you'd better find the fuse and disarm it, and not take all day about it, either.

I took a step toward her and she backed away, like a shadow backing away, and those eyes never looked at anything but my eyes. By God, I thought, I'm going to stop sticking pins in people, especially broads.

And that was when I pegged her.

Suddenly all the pieces fell into place, and I grinned. I had Dorris Venci pegged now, sure as hell!

I said, "What's wrong with you, Mrs. Venci?"

She didn't make a sound.

I took a step forward and she moved back until her back was against the wall. You could almost hear the scream in her eyes. I knew her little secret now, and it had been the simplest thing in the world, once I got the scent of it.

All I had to do was ask myself what kind of woman

was it that would go for John Venci, really go for him, not love him, necessarily? That was where I had been thrown off—confusing love with something else. Once I got back on the right track, the answer was simple. John Venci had been a tough boy; he had had a good, hard tough brain. Tough! So any woman who went for John Venci had to be a glutton for punishment. And that was the answer.

There was nothing new or unique about it; masochism is as old as Adam.

I said, "You look upset, Mrs. Venci. Why don't you sit down and take it easy for a minute."

She said, "Don't touch me! Don't *touch* me!"

"Gods don't die, Mrs. Venci," I said, "really they don't."

She made a small, thin sound—thinner than a spider's thread, harder than iron, and I grabbed her. I grabbed one shoulder and jerked her around, then I caught her wrist, twisting it behind her, and threw a hammer-lock on her. Her mouth snapped open and that thin little sound came out again as I put my back into it. I applied the pressure. I jerked up on her arm and jammed her clinched fist against the base of her skull.

She was very strong for a woman, and it was no easy matter keeping the hammer-lock on her. She fought like a tigress, hissing, cursing, clawing, and then she tramped down on my instep with the point of her French heel and I damn near tore her arm off at the shoulder.

"Don't!" she said, her voice sounding like it was being squeezed through a sieve. "Don't! Don't! Don't! ..." Then it trailed off and she began shuddering.

I had her hard against the wall now and she suddenly turned to jelly in my hands. She had no more strength or resistance than a pile of quivering flesh. I was completely fascinated with this transformation. Of course, I had heard about masochism, but this was the first time I ever walked up to it and looked it in the face.

When I put my back into that hammer-lock it was just like throwing a switch that set off a blast furnace. I could feel lust surge through her like a thousand volt shock. She gasped and closed her eyes and mashed herself against me, making little whimpering sounds, sounds like a whipped dog makes, a dog that is so completely broken that it is afraid to yelp.

I could have had her. There is absolutely no doubt about that; I could have had her but the phenomenon itself so completely fascinated me that I almost forgot for a while what it meant. But it crossed my mind, all right, you can bet your life on it. It wasn't because I didn't think of it that nothing happened.

It simply wouldn't be the smart thing to do—it would indicate that I needed her more than she needed me, and that would not do. I let her go.

She couldn't believe it. She stared at me, waiting, her breathing very shallow and rapid, and at last she realized that I was not following through. There was horror in her eyes. She leaned against the wall, she pressed her face to the wall, biting her lower lip as great tears spilled down her cheeks.

I said, "We learn something every day, don't we Mrs. Venci? Today we learned who's boss, isn't that right?" I took her arm again. "Isn't that right?"

She nodded. Quickly, eagerly, the instant I touched her.

"All right," I said. "You'd better relax; we've still got some business to talk over, remember?"

I went to the kitchen and had a glass of water. I thought: I hope she never finds out what that cost me!

I began to calm down, slowly. I rested against the kitchen sink and had another glass of water and after a while I felt pretty good, pretty proud of myself.

Yes sir, I thought, things are looking up. They certainly are! I had possessed her as completely as if I had laid her; I was boss now!

CHAPTER FIVE

I came into the sitting room and she was on the sofa, crumpled on the sofa like a discarded plaster manikin. "How about a glass of water?" I said.

She made no sound. The best thing to do, I decided, was let her alone until she pulled herself together. You think your nerves and glands took a beating, Surratt, I thought. Think what it must have done to hers! So I took a chair in the corner of the room and waited. I was in no hurry.

It gave me time to think, and I needed some time to think. Things were happening fast. It was about time to look around and see just where I was.

I had an angle now. I had a woman who was scared to death of her own abnormalities, who tried to cover them up, hide them, call them by strange names. A woman like that added up to an angle that a man could really get his fingers into. That was quite a beginning, considering that this was only my second day out of prison.

But it was only the beginning. An idea had been nibbling at the edge of my brain. Dorris had mentioned that her husband had set out to dispose of his enemies.... Now there was an angle to my liking, because John Venci had been much too polished to try anything as crude as murder. There was not much satisfaction in murder, it was too sudden—no, it would have been something else, it would have been something long-drawn-out and filled with anguish, the most exquisite anguish, I was sure, that it was possible to devise.

And that, of course, would be *mental* anguish.

Long-drawn-out and filled with anguish, that much fit perfectly, but how would the end eventually be achieved?

Then I had it. Venci had been nothing if not logical— self-destruction would have been his aim! Suicide!

I was on the right track now, I could feel it. Great mental anguish culminated by suicide—that would have appealed to John Venci. So the only thing left was the method with which he would achieve this end. One word came to my mind automatically—blackmail.

That was it! Venci had set out to blackmail his enemies, and that meant that he must have gone to fantastic lengths to gather evidence against them.

I grinned, feeling like a million dollars. All I had to do was get my hands on that evidence, and I had just the key to turn the lock! I had Dorris Venci! When I get through with this town, I thought, they'll think they've been hit by a hurricane!

I went over to the sofa and shook Dorris. "Okay," I said, "you ready to talk?"

She shuddered.

"Look," I said, "I'm not sure how we got off on this tangent, but I know one thing, it's time to get back on schedule. Go in the bathroom and wash your face or something."

When I was a kid I used to go out on the golf course and find golf balls. Just for the hell of it I would cut the golf balls open, cut deep into them, and the tightly-wound little bands of rubber would snap and writhe like something going crazy. The golf ball would go all to pieces right there in your hand. That's what Dorris reminded me of: she looked like she would go all to pieces any minute.

But she got up and went to the bathroom. After a while she came back and I was surprised to see that she was almost normal.

I said, "You were saying something about my killing somebody ..."

She glanced at me, her old icy self again. "I—I'm afraid I have changed my mind. I don't believe I need you, after all, Mr. Surratt."

"Like hell you don't need me," I said. "What do I have to do to convince you? You don't want to go through that act again, do you?"

That did it. She closed her eyes for a moment, her hands clenched hard, then she sank to the sofa.

"That's better," I said. "We understand each other, Dorris; I think we understand each other perfectly. We could make a hell of a pair, you and me, but it's going to take some cooperation from both of us."

"What is it you want?" she said tightly.

"Right now I want to get back where we left off."

"It isn't important now."

"It was important a few minutes ago, so it still is. You wanted somebody killed. I want to know who and I want to know why."

She knew I wasn't kidding. She glanced at me, then away. She put her hands in her lap and stared at them. "His name," she said at last, "is Alex Burton."

I whistled in surprise. "Alex Burton, the ex-governor of the state?"

She nodded, and I said, "Well, this is very interesting. Suppose you begin at the beginning." Then, before she could speak, I said, "Wait just a minute. I've been working on a hypothesis, and I want you to tell me if it's right."

So I told her my idea, the way I had it figured out. Her eyes widened when I began describing the scheme of blackmail and suicide.

"How did you know that!"

"It was just a guess," I said, "but a pretty sure one. Anyway, we can skip that part of it since I'm already familiar with it. Let's get down to the reasons for killing an ex-governor. Is he the one who killed your husband?"

She wanted to just sit there and say nothing, but she knew better than that. "... No," she said finally. "That is, I don't know, I'm not sure."

"Then why?"

"... Alex Burton wants to kill me."

I thought that one over, letting the picture take shape. "Uh-huh," I said, "that could make sense. Your husband was turning the screw on Burton. What he wanted was the dossier that Venci had gathered on him, some irrefutable evidence that would ruin Burton for good, especially in politics. So now Burton is trying to kill you, which means that he didn't get that dossier after all, which means that you have a pretty good idea where it is, or what's in it. Is that the way it is?"

She nodded, heavily.

"Where do you live?"

Only a moment's hesitation this time. She was beginning to come around, she was beginning to realize that I meant business. "208 Hunters Drive," she said flatly.

I gave the cab dispatcher the address and hung up. "Mrs. Venci," I said, "you can stop worrying about Alex Burton; I know how to take care of bastards like him. But I think we ought to have an understanding—there's going to be a fee."

She had recovered from her attack of female pride. Given time to think it over, even Dorris Venci could see that her chances of living were practically nil if Alex Burton wanted her dead—that is, unless I took care of Burton first. She said, "All right ... I'm willing to pay."

"You don't understand me," I said. "I want money, but not your money, not John Venci's money. I want that dossier that your husband collected on his enemies."

She stared hard at her hands. "And what ... do I get in return?"

"I told you, Mrs. Venci. I'll kill Burton before he kills you. You know you'll never be safe as long as you have those documents in your possession; actually, I'm doing you a favor by taking them."

Then she looked at me, and smiled the smallest, bitterest smile I ever saw. "I thought it would be so simple," she said, "when I helped you escape from prison. You would kill Alex Burton; I would give you a certain amount of money; and then you would leave the city and I would never see you again—that's the way I had planned it."

"Things are never as simple as they seem at first glance, Mrs. Venci. We'd better go now, the taxi's waiting."

"Wait a minute," she said, in a way that made me turn and look at her. "I agree to your ... proposition, but under two conditions. The first is that I am never to see you again, after you come into possession of the documents."

"That's fair enough. What's the second condition?"

"You don't get the documents until after the ... transaction has been completed."

I laughed. "Mrs. Venci, I was not born yesterday, not even the day before yesterday. This is strictly a pay-in-advance job we're talking about. Now, before we go," I said, "I want the answer to one question: Why did you take me out of the hotel and put me in this crummy apartment?"

She stood up, taking her lump gracefully enough about the advance payment. She said quietly, "Patricia Kelso lives just across the hall from you; she is Alex Burton's secretary."

"Is that supposed to help get me within killing distance of the ex-governor?"

"Where his secretary is, Alex Burton is not far behind."

I grinned. "Mrs. Venci," I said, "you have simplified things considerably. I apologize for some of the things I've been thinking about you."

CHAPTER SIX

"Ellen," Dorris Venci said, "show Mr. O'Connor to the library, will you, please?" Then, to me, "I'll be back in a few minutes."

"Sure," I said, watching her walk stiffly to a large spiral

stairway, then up the stairway, then out of sight.

Ellen, a grim, long-faced woman of about forty-five, said, "This way, Mr. O'Connor," and I followed her over the wide expanse of reddish carpeting, down a few steps, around some corners, and finally she opened a heavy mahogany door and stepped to one side. "Thank you," I said, walking into the library. The maid closed the door and vanished like yesterday's dreams.

It was a hell of a place, this place where the maestro had lived. Note it carefully, I thought, because this is the way you are going to live, Surratt. The king is dead—long live the king!

I stood there and tried to soak it up, the luxury of that room. The floor was of old oak, and a huge, thick carpet.

But there were other things on the wall, things to make a man's head swim, if he could even vaguely estimate their worth. For one thing there was a fantastically delicate Chinese tapestry, and there were paintings that I absolutely could not believe, *would not* believe to be originals, until I had inspected them closely. There was a large boating scene that I recognized as a Turner. On another wall there was an El Greco—*an* El Greco, mind you!

Those paintings so floored me that I forgot for a moment how fantastic it was finding them here in John Venci's library. But, when I did think about it, the answer was obvious. Paintings like that simply weren't for sale, not at any price. Possibly the Turner could have been bought—but not that El Greco, not in a hundred years! Those things were museum pieces, strictly!

The obvious implication just about bowled me over, By God, I thought, *he stole those things! John Venci stole them!*

The pure audacity of the thing struck me as being hilariously funny. I sank into a chair and felt the laughter coming up from my bowels! I lay back and howled.

The door opened, Dorris came into the room carrying a

small steel strongbox, and I was still laughing.

"What's so funny?"

"Those pictures," I said, trying to choke it down.

"Pictures?" She glanced at the paintings. "They never struck me as amusing."

I was off again. "How ... How long," I said, "have those paintings been here?"

"Why, for years."

"Did your husband keep this room locked? He didn't receive visitors in here, did he?"

"Of course he did; this was his favorite room. Now will you tell me why you're laughing?"

I said, "No. It would be a shame to spoil a joke as priceless as this one." In my mind I could see John Venci receiving governors, senators, bigshot politicians, all of them here in this room. I could see the cigar-chewing apes gaping about the room, seeing but uncomprehending, their brains as solid as concrete. I could appreciate the razor-sharp humor, the subtle, bitter hilarity that John Venci must have experienced as he watched their stupid faces. It was more than a wonderful, fantastic joke, it had been a source of fuel for the ego; it had been a day-by-day replenishment of confidence, for every time an oaf stared dumbly at those paintings, Venci's superiority was made brazenly obvious.

I stopped laughing and took the strongbox from Dorris. I could feel the transfer of power, John Venci's power becoming mine. *It's more than a strongbox,* I thought, *it's the world, and I've got it right in my hands. It is power over others and strength for myself, and I've got it right in my hands!*

"Is everything here?" I said.

"Yes."

"Then you won't mind if I look for myself, will you?"

She handed me the key and I opened the box. I was disappointed at first; there didn't seem to be much to it. The strongbox was arranged like a miniature filing cabinet and everything was very neat and orderly. The name on the first index card was *Allen, George W.*

I looked at Dorris. "Do you know a George W. Allen?"

"He is an insurance broker."

I skipped the material on Mr. Allen and turned up the next index card. "Karl Johnson Applewhite," I said. "President of the First National Bank."

That was more like it!

The next name was Alex Burton; and the next one was somebody named Colter, who Dorris said was merely a superintendent of one of the city schools. There were twenty index cards and I went through them quickly, having Dorris give me a quick rundown on each name. Some of the names I didn't have to ask about, they were known all over the state and even the nation. Some of the names meant absolutely nothing to me. A United States Senator or a down-at-the-heels school teacher, it had made no difference to John Venci. An enemy was an enemy, an old wound never healed. He had gone after the little ones just as relentlessly as he had the big ones.

And he had hooked them all. I didn't realize how completely he had hooked them until I started going through the material on a man named Kelton.

Kelton had been a pretty important boy. He had been a district attorney with one foot practically in the Governor's Mansion before John Venci had cut him down. It seems that the D.A. had somehow failed to summon an important witness in an important murder trial. The day after the trial the D.A. made a deposit of five thousand dollars and traded his Chevrolet in on a new Cadillac. Mr. Kelton had lost a murder trial, but obviously he had gained in other ways, and the proof was in the strongbox. A signed affidavit by the spurned witness, cancelled checks, bills of sale, plus a detailed account of Kelton's financial condition ten years back from the trial. As if that wasn't enough, there was also an affair with a certain young lady of doubtful reputation, to say the least, and this was backed up with photostats of hotel registers, actual photographs, bills of sale from various jewelry stores, clothing emporiums and even a liquor store. All this together with another signed affidavit from the young lady herself. Every bit of evidence was strong almost to the point of ridiculousness, and any one bit would have brought him crashing from his political heights, and many of them would have landed him long prison terms.

Mr. Kelton was cooked. He had known that he was cooked. First his wife had divorced him, then there were rumors of grand jury investigations. The rest of it was spelled out in a newspaper clipping, also included in the material on Kelton. The headline was: D.A. KILLED IN FREAK AUTOMOBILE ACCIDENT.

It didn't come right out and say that it had been suicide, but that wasn't important: John Venci had known.

All in all there were four names that I couldn't use at all because Venci had already finished them off. One was killed in another "freak" automobile accident, another took too many sleeping pills, and the third, who didn't have the guts to kill himself, was suddenly discovered to have played a leading role in a seven-year-old murder and drew life in the State penitentiary.

Quickly, I ran down some of the other material, especially the material that John Venci had gathered on Alex Burton. Most of the stuff on the ex-governor was in photostatic form, photostats of bills of sale, cancelled checks, deposit slips, and even photostats of Burton's income tax forms for five years back. The upshot of the evidence was that Burton had made himself a killing running well into six figures during the four year stretch he had put in at the State Capitol. It was rock-hard, iron-bound evidence that could put Burton so far back in prison that they'd have to pump air to him.

It was incredible, it was almost more than I could believe, but it was there, it sure was!

Dorris Venci said, "Are you satisfied?"

"Perfectly. It's pretty hard to swallow all at once, it's something I'll have to chew on for a while before I can digest it. But I'm satisfied, all right, in spades."

"... And Alex Burton," she asked flatly.

It was almost a shame to kill a man like that when I had all that evidence on him—still, he had proved that he was dangerous. He sure had proved it to John Venci. Yes, I thought, the only smart way to handle it is to kill Burton. There were still plenty of fish left, and I had plenty of bait.

I said, "You can stop worrying about Burton, Mrs. Venci."

"I hope you realize it won't be easy."

"Please relax," I said. "Just keep out of sight for a day or two; I won't let him kill you."

But she wasn't so sure about that.

I said, "Look, Mrs. Venci, I'm no amateur, this is no punk kid trying to work up his guts to stick up an oil station, this is a professional, a well trained professional playing for big stakes. I'm not underrating Burton—a man with his record has to be pretty smart, but I've handled smart boys before, and I can do it again. So take it easy."

I was half afraid that she would let her natural female instability lead her into some unpredictable action that would ruin everything. I was sorry now that I had got rough with her. She still knew things, she was still Mrs. John Venci, and I could use her on my side.

"Good-by," she said.

"Oh ... Yes, I guess I've been here long enough. But before I go, is there anything you want to tell me, about Burton, I mean?"

"... No. You said you could handle it."

"So I did. Well, I'll be going."

She rang for the maid. We stood there looking at each other, and after a moment she said, "I really mean good-by. Don't ever try to see me again, ever."

Not until I got back to my apartment did I remember Dorris had brought a package with her that morning. The package was still in the kitchen where she had left it, partly unwrapped. I opened it up and the first thing I saw was a nicely blued, but not new, "police special" .38 caliber revolver. There was also a box of ammunition. But the thing that caught my eye was the money. There was a package of fives, a package of tens and a package of twenties, every bill brand new and crisp and green.

I counted it out and it came to five hundred on the nose.

Well, I thought, this is very nice. This is very nice of you, Mrs. Venci. You may be a little mixed up sexually, but what's an aberration or so among friends—you've got your nice side, too. Yes sir, you sure have!

I pocketed the money and went out to find the biggest goddamn steak in Lake City.

CHAPTER SEVEN

I was at the mail box in the hallway next morning when she came out of her apartment. She was just about the handsomest girl I ever saw, this Pat Kelso, this secretary of Alex Burton's that Dorris Venci had hinted was something more than a secretary. She walked like royalty: chin up, erect, every step sure and solid.

"Good morning," I said.

She smiled faintly. "Good morning."

"Pardon me, but could you tell me what time the postman comes around? I'm new to this neighborhood." Then I added, "I just moved in yesterday, down the hall. Apartment seven."

I thought maybe she would say something about our being neighbors, but she didn't. "I believe the postman comes later," she said, "around ten." Then she nodded pleasantly, smiled that faint smile again, and walked out of the building.

I went to the door and watched her walk to the curb where a taxi was waiting. Pat Kelso. The name stuck with me, and the vision stuck with me. This girl is class, I told myself. How did she ever get mixed up with a bastard like Burton?

Then I remembered that most people didn't know Burton as I now knew him. After all, he was a very wealthy and powerful and respected man in the state. He was a bigshot; he was an ex-governor. Maybe that's the kind of guy girls with class went for. I watched her as she got into the cab. Pat Kelso, I thought, I think we ought to get better acquainted.

The telephone was ringing when I got back to the apartment. Words jumped out at me when I picked up the receiver, frightened words coming fast and making no sense at all. It was Dorris Venci and she was scared.

"Hold it, Mrs. Venci," I said. "Now what's the trouble?"

"A man tried to kill me!"

"Who? When?"

"I don't know who, just a man, one of Alex Burton's men, it could have been anybody. But he isn't important, Alex Burton is the important one. Have ... have you done ..."

"Not yet," I said. "After all it's only been a few hours; I've got to have a little time to figure something out."

"Something's got to be done!"

"It sure has," I said. "You've got to get hold of yourself. Now calm down and tell me what happened."

"I told you, a man tried to kill me! It was last night, this morning, rather, about two o'clock. I woke up and there he was in my room; he had a gun!"

"Hold on. How did he get in your room? You had the house locked, didn't you?"

"Yes, the house was locked, but there's latticework and vines on the north side, and he must have used that to climb up to the second floor. He broke a window—rather *cut* the window, a small hole near the lock—that was how he got in."

"I see. Then what happened."

"I woke up and there he was. He had a gun pointed right at me!"

I said, "I don't get it. If he went to that trouble and had a gun pointed at you, why didn't he kill you?"

"He tried, that's what I'm trying to tell you. He fired once but I had thrown myself off the bed. Luckily, before he could find me in the dark, Ellen began knocking on my door, making an awful noise, and I guess that's what frightened him away."

"You mean he just knocked off the job and left? I'd hate to hire a man like that."

"I told you that Ellen was making a lot of noise, and, besides, she had a gun. She finally got the door open and fired once. Of course the killer couldn't see who it was; he fired once more in the darkness and left."

"How did he get out of the house?"

"He jumped from my window, my bedroom window."

"Then there's one hell of a sore hoodlum somewhere in Lake City this morning, taking a drop like that. But it's over now. The main thing is for you to calm down and be quiet, and keep Ellen quiet too. I'll think of something."

"Soon!"

"All right, soon."

"Today! Tonight at the latest!"

"All right, I said I would take care of it. Calm down."

"There's one more thing," she said. "My safe was open, the wall safe upstairs where the strongbox was kept."

I whistled. "That was close; I got that stuff just in time.

And you are right about Burton, the bastard is entirely too persistent. Well, he won't be so persistent this time tomorrow. Just think about that and try to get some sleep."

I hung up.

That goddamn Burton, I thought, he's going to ruin things good if I don't stop him. When a politician gets in so deep that he starts playing with murder, that was the time to do one of two things: either back off fast and get out of the blast area when the explosion comes, or close in fast and try to get at the fuse.

There was one thing I was sure of—I wasn't backing away. I had my hands on a million dollars worth of blackmail material. So Burton had to go, and fast. Soon as he found out that Dorris no longer had the evidence, he'd come after me. Somehow he would find out about me. That's the only trouble with blackmailing—sooner or later you run into a guy like Burton, a guy who won't give.

So, right on the spot, I made up my mind about Burton. I was going to kill him today, or tonight—anyway, within the next twelve hours—if it was humanly possible. But it wasn't going to be easy. I didn't know a thing about his personal habits, except he was somehow tied up with his secretary, Pat Kelso. That was the angle I would have to use, it was the only angle I had.

The only thing to do was begin at the beginning and try to find out something about Pat Kelso. I had a look at the door across the hall, the door to Pat Kelso's apartment, hoping that it would be unlocked, but of course it wasn't. That didn't stop me for long.

I went back and looked at my own door and smiled a little when I saw that it was equipped with an ordinary spring-operated night latch. In my kitchen I found a cheap paring knife, a flexible, stainless steel affair that was practically made to order.

I made sure that the hallway was empty, then went to work on Miss Kelso's night latch. The blade went in easily.

I bent the knife toward the door and forced the point down the sloping shoulder of the spring bolt. When the point of the knife reached the leading edge of the bolt, I bent the blade the other way and the stronger tension of the steel blade snapped the spring-actuated bolt back into the latch body and the door was open. I stepped inside and closed the door behind me.

The apartment was much like mine but neater. It was almost mannish in its neatness and simplicity.

I walked into the bedroom and this too was neat and simple: tweed at the windows, fruitwood furniture which was not expensive but too expensive to belong to the apartment. I started going through a chest of drawers and found nothing but lingerie, but there was a silver-framed photograph on top of the chest that interested me. It was a man of about fifty-five or so, a square-jawed, blunt-featured man with bristling gray hair, and a rather grim mouth that was bent determinedly up at the corners in something that might pass as a smile. Just for the hell of it I took the picture out of the frame, and there on the back scrawled in bold, blunt letters, was: "For Pat, with all my love, Alex."

It was strange, the way that picture affected me. Until that moment Alex Burton had been an abstraction, an inanimate obstacle that had been placed in my path and which had to be removed. Now it was different. The longer I looked at that picture, the more I hated the man it represented, and I didn't know exactly why, except that I resented the presence of that picture and its implications. I simply couldn't see a girl like Pat Kelso with a man like Burton. I thought of the girl I had seen at the mail box, then I looked at the picture, and I looked at the bed in Pat Kelso's room, and the three of them came together in my mind.

With that picture in my hand, I thought: You sonofabitch, you lousy sonofabitch! Without even knowing what I was angry about.

At last I put the picture back in the frame. I made myself settle down. I got out of that bedroom.

Stop it, Surratt! What kind of insanity is this, anyway, getting yourself steamed up just because another secretary decides it's more convenient to sleep with the boss than look for another job? She's just another broad, Surratt, and a broad you hardly even know, at that. So forget her. Think about the job at hand—that ought to keep you busy.

It was good advice. And I took it. When a man starts thinking with his glands instead of his brain he's sunk, and I realized that I had been doing exactly that. I had been too damn long without a woman. After all, I was human, I was a man. Any other man would react the same way, I thought, after five years of celibacy.

I was convinced.

"It is perfectly normal and completely glandular," I said aloud.

I went back to the sitting room and got into action with the telephone directory. In the white pages I found Burton, and then I moved down to Burton Finance and Loans, and dialed the number. After a moment a blatantly nasal voice bleated: "Burtonfinanceandloans!"

"I want to talk to Miss Kelso. Pat Kelso."

"Sorrynooneherebythatname!"

I hung up and moved down to Burton Manufacturing and Construction Company. This time the voice was pleasant and professionally precise.

I said, "I want to talk to Miss Kelso."

"Miss Kelso is on the other line, sir. Would you like to ..."

I hung up.

Now I had a starting place.

CHAPTER EIGHT

The first thing I did was rent a black Chevrolet sedan from a U-Drive-It place which I found in the telephone directory. Then I started looking for the Burton Manufacturing and Construction Company.

It turned out to be a sprawling brick building, and several smaller buildings, south of the city in the factory district. I circled the place slowly, looking it over, and finally found a parking place in front of the main building where the office workers would come out. Then I settled down to wait.

This was the tedious way of getting at Burton, but it was the only way. One thing I was sure of, I wasn't going to stalk the lion in his lair, I wasn't going to elbow my way through hired bodyguards, hoodlums and flunkies to get at him—I was going to let Alex Burton come to me. I hoped he would come to me today, but if he didn't, I could wait. I was going to sit here and wait for Pat Kelso to come out of that building, and then I was going to follow her to the end of the line.

Sooner or later it would lead me to Burton. More than that, it would lead me to Burton when he was most vulnerable. I knew these men like Alex Burton, these bigshots who like to throw their weight around but deep inside are scared in their guts. Because they are scared they hire themselves a pair of hotshots from Chicago, or Detroit, or some place, and they place armed guards and electric fences around their homes, and they tell themselves they are safe. No matter how many enemies they make, they are safe. Or so they think.

But they are vulnerable. There are situations in which they have to stand on their own feet, naked and alone.

With women, they are vulnerable. I never heard of one, no matter how great a coward he was, who prepared himself for a lady's bedroom by flanking himself with bodyguards.

Oh, yes, they were vulnerable, all right, if you only waited.

I waited.

Noon came and only a scattering of people came out of the building. I went on waiting. The afternoon crawled by and my stomach growled for food and my throat was dry, but I didn't dare leave that car. There was always a chance that Pat would leave for some reason, or that Burton would pick her up, and I wanted to be on hand if anything like that happened.

But nothing happened. There was a big parking area behind the main building and I watched the single exit like a hawk ... still, nothing happened. Then, around four o'clock a squadron of taxi cabs began lining up in front of the building and I knew the time of waiting was about over. Soon I would know if today would be the day, or if I would have to do it again.

Another fifteen minutes passed. A ridiculously long, black limousine slipped into the street and moved like a huge shadow between the files of parked traffic. The back seat was empty. As the limousine slid past me and turned into the entrance gate of the company parking lot I studied the driver. He was in full livery, a beefy, flat-faced kid of about twenty-three or -four with *punk* written all over him. He yelled something to one of the parking attendants, then drove on around to the back of the building and out of sight. I turned my attention back to the main entrance of the building, where the office workers would soon be coming out.

I almost missed that limousine as it slipped out of the parking lot and headed up the street in the opposite direction. If it hadn't been so big and black I would have missed it altogether—but it was pretty hard to miss a thing that big. I turned my head just in time to see that there was somebody in the back seat this time. All I could see was the passenger's head, but that was enough. The passenger was Pat Kelso.

Well, I thought, slamming the Chevy into gear, Miss Kelso believes in traveling first class, I'll say that for her. I pulled out in the middle of the street and finally got the Chevy headed in the direction the limousine was going.

The limousine headed right toward the heart of town, me in the Chevy about a block behind. No use sticking too close, there wasn't much chance losing an automobile as big as that one. We hit a four lane expressway and everything was clear sailing—I breathed a little faster when we crossed North Hampton and kept on going. It meant Pat Kelso wasn't going home; that meant that Burton had sent his limousine to pick her up and now she was going to meet him. Surratt, I thought, this is your lucky day.

The University Club was right in the middle of town, a red brick and white limestone monstrosity. Just beyond the main entrance to the club there was a drive-in entrance with a sign over it: UNIVERSITY CLUB GARAGE. MEMBERS ONLY. Directly in front of the main entrance there were two sidewalk signs which read: NO PARKING. NO STANDING. The curb between the two signs was painted red and there was white stenciled lettering standing boldly against that red background. NO PARKING AT ANY TIME. The punk chauffeur blandly ignored the garage, the sidewalk no-parking signs, the red curb and white lettering, and parked the limousine against the curb.

A uniformed doorman burst out of the University Club and had the limousine door open almost immediately. He showed his teeth, he grinned, he bowed, he helped Pat Kelso out of the limousine as though he were assisting a very aged and crippled queen, and finally, after he had done his job to perfection, he stood, head bowed, looking heart-broken because there was no other way he could help her.

It was really quite a show. I only glimpsed it as I eased the Chevrolet up the street, but I got the idea.

I circled the block two times and finally found an open space and slipped the Chevy in next to a parking meter. Five o'clock.

I got out of the Chevy and strolled down to a cigar store next to the University Club garage. That limousine was still there in the no parking zone. The punk was out stretching his legs. He took a swipe or two at the gleaming hood with a dust cloth, then went over to one of the sidewalk signs and leaned on it insolently, dragging on a cigarette.

He was some boy, that chauffer, cocky as a Marine. A cop strolled by, making a great business of not seeing the limousine in the no parking zone, which was no easy feat. The punk grinned. He looked as though he had just pulled the Brink's robbery single handed.

I strolled back up the street to a bootblack stand that I had noticed.

"Shine 'em up, mister?"

"Sure."

From my perch on the shine bench I could still see the limousine and the chauffeur. The boy went to work on my shoes, and I scanned the front page of the paper for something on the prison escape story, but nothing was there. On page eight there was a quarter column quoting the warden as saying I didn't have a chance. They knew all my old contacts, all my friends, and it was just a matter of time before I would have to get in touch with them. The police had several leads that were too hot for publication—which is what they always said when they knew absolutely nothing.

I read the escape story through and felt fine. My old contacts were a thousand miles from Lake City. As for friends, I hadn't any. Roy Surratt against the world, I liked it that way. Not even John Venci had been a friend. I had admired his brain. He had dazzled me with criminal theory and his tremendous knowledge of criminal philosophy. I had been greatly impressed with his logical approach to crime, for, until I met John Venci, I had believed that I was the only modern criminal in existence who had actually developed a workable, livable criminal philosophy based entirely on logic.

I had been wrong. John Venci had worked it out before me. "There you are, sir!" the shine boy said.

I gave him a dollar and said, "Keep the change."

"Yes *sir!* Thank you, *sir!*" He grinned, pocketed the money, gave my shoes a couple of extra licks just to show he was doing a good job.

I went out on the sidewalk, glanced toward the limousine. The punk had shifted over to the other no-parking sign and was busy leering at the white-collar girls waiting at the corner bus stop. I walked over to him and said, "Say, that's quite an automobile you've got here. I was just noticing it."

"Look, bo," the amateur Bogart said from the corner of his mouth, "I got no time to stand here an' chew the rag with every farmer come by. You better move on."

"I just want to ..."

"I ain't interested," he said, "Now move on before I get annoyed."

Why, you simian sonofabitch, I thought, you make one move in my direction, just one single move, and you'll be till sundown gathering your teeth off the sidewalk. I stood there for a full thirty seconds, almost hoping that he would start something.

All he did was sweat. He didn't know what to do. The comic books don't tell you what to do in a case like that. I flicked a small ash from his whipcord jacket, then he blinked as I jabbed my forefinger into his soler plexus and fanned my thumb like a Hollywood gunfighter. "I enjoyed the chat, Humphrey. Maybe I'll run into you again, sometime."

I walked to the cigar store and looked back. The punk seemed a bit disturbed. He tried leaning on the no-parking sign, but it wasn't the same as it had been before. Finally he gave it up and got back in the limousine.

I moved up the street, pausing at store windows, killing all the time I could. How long were Burton and his secretary going to stay in that club, anyway? Were they just having cocktails, or were they staying for dinner, or what? I sure couldn't wait for them on the sidewalk and burn Burton down when they came out, although the pure audacity of that fleeting thought did appeal to my sense of the bizarre. No, I thought, this has got to be fast and it has got to be bold, but not *that* bold!

Finally, I saw them cross the sidewalk. Alex Burton, a little heavier than I would have guessed from that photograph, a little softer looking. Pat Kelso had one arm in Burton's and she was smiling at whatever Burton was saying. She was absolutely the most beautiful woman I ever saw. And it wasn't only because I had been five years without a woman!

CHAPTER NINE

I was in the Chevy and had the motor going by the time Burton and his secretary got themselves settled in the limousine. I slipped in behind them, about three cars back, when they came past me. The punk tooled the black job through the heavy traffic as though he were behind the controls of a Patton tank, stopping for red lights only when it pleased him, and I had a hell of a time keeping him in sight until finally he slipped back on the expressway. Then I closed the gap.

I had no idea where we were going, except that we were

headed away from the city, going north. Maybe, I thought, Burton has a house out here somewhere. If that's the case, I'm sunk. I sure wasn't going to have any luck getting close to Burton on his home field.

Then my heart swelled just a little as the limousine turned off the expressway. I hung back as far as possible, thinking, now we'll find out. The limousine turned again, off a paved street onto a graveled road. When I reached the corner in the Chevy, I grinned. This was more like it. The cards were falling in my direction.

There was a brick pillar on the turn-off. On the pillar there was a bronze plaque with raised lettering: CRESTVIEW CLUB. MEMBERS ONLY.

A formal stand of cypress shielded the Crestview Club from the paved street, and a stone wall jealously guarded it on the side of the graveled road. I cruised by at a normal speed after the limousine had turned in, and right away I realized that this place was out of the question. There were two uniformed attendants at the big wrought iron entrance gate, and farther down, at the end of the stone wall, there was another attendant, or guard. This goddamn place, I thought, is only slightly less guarded than Fort Knox! Which could mean just one thing—there was gambling going on inside, big-money gambling, and the management was taking no chances on a heist.

It looked like a fine place, just the kind of club Alex Burton would belong to, and a hell of a place to crash. I had seen enough to know that it couldn't be crashed, not by one man, anyway, so I drove on until I came to a dirt section line road, then circled the entire section and came back on the paved street to the brick pillar.

The club was out.

As long as Burton stayed in that place I couldn't reach him with a 37 millimeter cannon. But the night wasn't over yet.

I nosed the Chevy off the pavement onto the club crossroad, but in the opposite direction. This end of the road was not graveled, since it apparently led to nowhere. I traveled for maybe a quarter mile between heavy stands of trees, then turned the car around and headed toward the pavement, facing the paved street and the club. About a hundred yards from the street I pulled the Chevy on a rutted shoulder, in the long shadows, and stopped.

I would wait. I would wait and watch that road, and when the limousine came out I would follow it right to the end of the line. There was no sense beating my brains out on something I couldn't whip, it was much easier to wait. Sooner or later I would find an opening. Sooner or later Burton would relax.

I checked the .38 that Dorris Venci had left for me. I checked the double action mechanism, the cylinder rotating mechanism, and the firing pin. I took five cartridges from the sealed box, wiped the cartridges carefully with my handkerchief and slipped them into the cylinder. I rotated the cylinder until the one empty chamber was in firing position and I eased the hammer down on it. The extra cartridges I dropped into my coat pocket; the .38 went into my waistband where it was convenient and stood little chance of becoming fouled with lint.

I waited.

Dusk became darkness, and I could see the misty lights of the club.

Seven, eight, nine o'clock.

I waited.

Nine, ten, ten-thirty. I had no watch but I could hear those out-of-tune electronic chimes banging out each quarter hour, so I knew what time it was, although I tried not to listen.

Eleven o'clock, eleven-fifteen.

I checked the .38 again just to give my hands something to do. Eleven-thirty. I saw the limousine turn off the graveled road and onto the highway. If my chance was coming tonight, it would be soon. I waited until the limousine had passed, then switched my lights on and followed.

After all the tailing and waiting and hoping, it seemed anti-climactic that the actual business of killing Burton should be so easy. Once more we took the expressway to town, and then the limousine turned west on North Hampton Street and I thought: By God, I've been doing all this tail chasing for nothing! We were headed right back where I started from. The apartment building.

I switched off my lights and coasted to the curb about a block behind the limousine. I saw Burton and Pat Kelso get out of the car, and I saw the chauffeur standing there holding the door open for them. Burton and his secretary started up to walk to the front entrance. I headed for the limousine.

I stuck my head in the door and said, "Whataya know, Humphrey? I had a feeling we might meet again some-time."

At first he just looked surprised. Then he recognized me and began to get mad. I guess he had been thinking about our chat in front of the University Club. He had it all planned out in his mind just how he was going to tell me off if he ever saw me again, but before he could say any-thing I stuck the .38 in his face. I put it right under his nose where he could smell the gun oil and steel.

"What the hell is this!"

"Nothing yet," I said, getting into the back seat. "Just stay where you are. Don't move or make a sound."

"By God, if you think ... !"

I jammed the muzzle into his throat and he almost fainted. "Listen to me, punk, and listen good! I want you to sit there like a goddamn statue. You move one muscle and I'll blow the roof of your mouth through your skull!"

He could be a very smart boy when it suited him. He didn't move a muscle. He sat just like a statue. I leaned over the back of the seat, moving the muzzle of the .38

until it was pressing against the base of his skull, then I patted him down. He wore a .38 automatic in a shoulder holster, just like in the movies. His only trouble was that automatic might as well have been a chocolate bar, for all the good it had done him. He hadn't even made a move in its direction.

I never cared for automatics. There are too many things to go wrong with them. I shoved it in my coat pocket, then reached back with one hand and pulled down the folding jump seat by the door.

"If it's money," he said tightly, "I ain't got any."

"It isn't money," I said.

"What is it, then? For God's sake, what is it?"

"All right, Humphrey," I said, "I'll tell you what it is. I'm going to kill your boss. When he comes out of that apartment building, you're going to just sit there behind the wheel and say nothing and do nothing. Is that clear?"

"Kill Mr. Burton? Why?"

"I've got my reasons, Humphrey."

"For Christ's sake, Mr. Burton's the finest guy in the world! Why in the world would you want to kill him?"

"He's so goddamn nice, why does he dress his chauffeur in a .38?"

"Jeez, for protection!"

I laughed. "A fine lot of protection he's going to get out of you, Humphrey. I wouldn't be at all surprised if you didn't lose your job over this."

He was sweating plenty. I kept grinding the muzzle of my revolver into the back of his neck and I could see the nervous sweat oozing out on his face.

"Jeez, won't you take that thing out of my neck!"

"Sorry, Humphrey, it's necessary. It's a reminder of what will happen to you if you should feel any hero impulse coming on."

He sat very still and quiet for several minutes, and so did I. After a while I heard a soft hiss, a bare whisper of a hiss, and then I recognized it as the vacuum stop on the apartment building's front door. Then a figure grew out of the darkness, heading toward the limousine.

"Remember, Humphrey."

He whimpered a little. A very small whimper.

Then suddenly the night was alive with noise. The twin air horns on that limousine exploded a steady stream of sound into the darkness. I jerked my pistol out of Humphrey's neck and clubbed him with the barrel. I hit him again and again, and finally the noise of the horns stopped as abruptly as it had begun. I jumped out of the car and almost ran over Burton.

"Listen," I said, jamming the revolver hard into his gut, "you make one sound and you're dead! You understand that?"

"What ... What's going on here! Where's Robert!"

"If Robert's your chauffeur he's nursing a fractured skull. Now get in under the wheel and do it quick!"

"No!" His eyes were wild. He was completely panic stricken. He tried to shove himself away from me, and I knew immediately that it would have to be done here and now.

To muffle the sound I jammed the muzzle hard into his soft stomach—still the noise sounded like a TNT plant going up when I pulled the trigger. Burton's mouth flew open. He started clawing at his middle, but that action was pure reflex. Alex Burton had died almost instantly.

His body was a hell of a thing to handle. He had weighed almost two hundred pounds and there didn't seem to be any place to grab hold. However, I did manage to get him in the back seat and close the door. Then I got under the wheel of the limousine, after shoving Humphrey down to the floorboards, and got away from there. It seemed incredible to me that the street wasn't filled with people—horns blasting, guns exploding!

The noise, I guess, hadn't been nearly as loud as it had

seemed to me, but it had been plenty loud enough.

For a moment all I could think of was getting away from that neighborhood as fast as possible, but soon I began to settle down. The excitement and wildness, the exhilaration born of sudden violence, began to cool in my brain and I thought: Hold it, Surratt! This is no time to risk a reckless driving charge, not with a dead man in the car, an ex-governor at that! Maybe a dead ex-governor and a dead chauffeur as well.

Traffic was pretty thin on the side streets at that time of night, and I kept going south and east, not knowing where I was going, but knowing that I had to get that limousine and the bodies as far away from the apartment as possible. Pretty soon we were in the factory district again, not far from Burton's own plant, and I decided that this would be as good a place as any. This part of town was drab, dead and lifeless at this time of night; the buildings standing gaunt and empty-eyed. I turned into a narrow brick paved street, a private one-way street that would be jammed in the daytime with trucks loading and unloading at one of the factories, but now it was empty.

I stopped the limousine and listened. There was no sound at all in the immediate neighborhood. Only then did I examine the chauffeur. He was dead.

With my handkerchief I wiped the steering wheel, the dash, the doors, the windows, everything I might have touched. Then I wiped Humphrey's automatic and left it on the front seat—I had no use for automatics, and it wouldn't have been smart to keep it if I had.

I had one good look at Burton before I left. He didn't look like much. His mouth was open, as though he was trying to yell, and his eyes were open, very wide. He looked like the most surprised bastard in the world.

I felt pretty good.

It had come off very nicely. The one man in Lake City who had had the power and brains to buck John Venci was dead. It was clear sailing now; the single danger had been eliminated. I said aloud, "Sweet dreams, boys," and walked away.

I turned west and saw a bar at the end of the block. Up ahead, in the middle of the next block there was an all night eating place—I went in and ordered a glass of milk and a piece of pie. Later I called a taxi, and when he arrived I gave the driver an address downtown. Downtown I took another cab and went to an address southeast, and from there I took still another cab to within a couple of blocks of my apartment. It took some time, but it would be worth it when the cops went to work.

It was about one o'clock when I finally walked into my apartment. I had company.

It was Dorris Venci.

I said, "Well, for a woman who never wanted to see me again, you pop up in some pretty strange places."

"I had to know!" she said quickly. "Did you ... ?"

"I did."

"... Oh."

I closed the door, walked into the room and dropped into a chair. She sat on the sofa with her hands clasped in her lap, every muscle in her body as rigid as steel. "Are ... Are you sure?" she said nervously.

"I give you my personal guarantee; you can stop worrying about Burton's hoodlums coming in your windows and you can stop worrying about being killed.

"Relax, now. You're going to fly all to pieces one of these days if you don't learn how to relax." I was tired. It had been a very successful day, but it had also been a wearing one. "Why don't you go home," I said, "and try to get some sleep?"

She stared at her hands. "Yes ... I suppose I should."

But she didn't move.

"Well," I said, "you might as well come out with it."

"What?"

"You didn't come here just to find out about Burton. All you had to do was lift the phone; I would have told you. No, you came here because you've got something on your mind, so what is it?"

She looked at me. "Don't you know?"

Suddenly I wasn't as tired as I thought I was. Still, there was caution in the back of my brain and it kept nudging me.

"Yes," she said flatly, "You know. And John. The only two people in the world who knew, or guessed, or could ... satisfy ... this awful sickness in my soul."

"It's not as monstrous as you think," I said. "Matter of fact, it is fairly common."

More than anything in the world she wanted to run. She wanted to run from the apartment, from me, from herself most of all, but she couldn't move.

I knew what the end of this was going to be. I didn't know if it was smart, and at that moment I didn't care, but the longer I looked at Dorris Venci the more desirable she became. She was really a hell of a woman, especially at a time like this.

I stared at her and could think of nothing else. The vision of Pat Kelso was swept from my brain completely and a bright blue flame took its place. I grabbed her arm, just below the wrist joint, and began to squeeze. I dug my fingers in the most sensitive area, between the two flexor tendons, and applied sharp pressure to the median nerve.

Her reaction was instant and violent. The shock went through her, shook her. She came off the couch and threw herself at me. "Now! Now!"

CHAPTER TEN

The newspapers made a hell of a racket about the Burton killing. I had expected headlines, and maybe even a front page editorial, but I hadn't expected anything like what really happened. For a whole week there was nothing but Alex Burton.

According to newspaper editorialists and radio commentators, St. Francis of Assisi had been an outright scoundrel, compared to Alex Burton. A feature story on Burton's life ran to twelve installments. Preachers made him a martyr, used him as a subject for a number of sermons. A song writer composed something called *Alex Burton, Friend Of The Common Man.* A citizens' committee was formed and issued an ultimatum to the police department: get Alex Burton's murderer, or else!

The craziest thing about the whole affair, though, was that every man, woman and child in Lake City believed every word they read or heard concerning the late Alex Burton. They thought of him as a kindly man who loved children, headed charity organizations, gave Thanksgiving and Christmas baskets to the needy; they thought of him as a tower of righteousness and strength. They thought of him as being on just one small step below God Himself!

Not only after his death, which might be explained as emotional hysteria, but they had believed it while he was alive! They had begged him to run for a second term as Governor—this thieving, knavish, pompous bastard who had robbed them blind during his political lifetime, had bled the State white, had committed every crime in the book, including murder, and I had the evidence to prove it! It was incredible that a man could have duped so many people so thoroughly, but Alex Burton had managed it.

All in all, it rather amused me. This hullabaloo was the most damaging comment imaginable on the intellect of the common herd. John Venci, too, would have appreciated a joke like this.

From John Venci's strongbox I selected the name of Parker King, a wealthy state senator, to go to work on. Politicians are easier to convince than most men; they have more to be afraid of. So Senator King seemed an excellent prospect. At the same time, as I looked into King's background, there was Dorris Venci who had to reckoned with. The task was not unpleasant, not in the least, so long as we kept it purely biological. And, too, there was Pat Kelso.

For me, Pat completed the circle. King promised the prospect of violence that I had to have to feel alive. Dorris offered biological satisfaction which I needed to keep my brain honed to the necessary sharpness. Pat Kelso ... she was everything else.

I went after her.

"Why, hello there!"

I had tried several things since Burton's funeral: A few words at the mailbox, brief, senseless conversations in the hallway of our apartment building. Those tactics hadn't got me anywhere, so I had come right out to the Burton factory where she still worked.

It was quitting time and she had come out with all the other office workers this time. No chauffeur to pick her up in a limousine and whisk her off to the University Club. Burton's death had brought Pat Kelso down in the world somewhat, but it hadn't brought her off her queenly bearing.

I said, "Remember me? I'm your neighbor. William O'-Connor from across the hall."

"... Oh, yes, " smiling faintly. "I didn't know you worked here, Mr. O'Connor."

I laughed. "I don't work here, I just came out to see a

friend who does. Charlie Burkett, in Advertising. Maybe you know him."

"No, I'm afraid I don't." We were standing on the sidewalk in front of the building, the white-collar parade going past on either side.

"Miss Kelso," I said, and she paused for a moment, half turning. "I was just thinking, Miss Kelso, I'm going back to the apartment myself."

No smile this time. "I'm sorry, Mr. O'Connor, I'd rather...."

She left it hanging, nodded, then walked on by herself. Well, by God, I thought, this kind of thing has got to stop! I'm getting pretty goddamn tired of women looking at me like I was something pickled in formaldehyde. I followed her.

I said, "All right, I didn't come out here to see a friend, and I never knew a Charlie Burkett."

Anyway, it stopped her, it surprised her. "I beg your pardon?"

"Miss Kelso," I said, "don't you think it's about time you joined the Living?"

She frowned, "Really, Mr. O'Connor, I don't know ..."

"Yes, you do," I said. "I've tried just about everything in the book to get to know you better, and finally I tried this; you know it."

People were staring at us, and that bothered her. I took her arm and helped her into a waiting taxi, then got in beside her. I said to the driver, "The Lake Hotel," then settled back and looked at her.

She was not afraid, merely curious. "You are very persuasive person, Mr. O'Connor," she said dryly.

"Yes, I can be persuasive if the occasion calls for it."

Unsmiling, she looked at me, strangely, as though she was seeing me for the first time. She said, "What did you mean when you said it was time I joined the Living?"

"It's pretty obvious to an interested observer. You haven't

been anywhere, seen anybody, you haven't even smiled since Alex Burton was killed."

She looked as though I had slapped her. "Relax," I said. It seemed that I was always telling women to relax. "It's not exactly a secret, is it, that Alex Burton and his secretary were ..."

"I'll thank you," she hissed, "to keep out of my life, Mr. O'Connor!"

I shrugged.

"And I'm not going to the Lake Hotel with you, or anywhere else! I'm going home!"

"I had hoped I wouldn't have to bring this up," I said, "but you leave me no alternative. It's a little awkward for me; for a while I thought about telling it to the police, but then I thought what the hell, there's no use spoiling a nice girl's life." I grinned. "You *are* a nice girl, aren't you, Miss Kelso?"

She didn't know what I was getting at, but she was doing some pretty fast guessing, and she didn't like it. I said, "It was pure accident, understand, that I happened to see Burton entering your apartment just about the time he was killed, according to the police coroner. After all, we are neighbors, and a person does get curious about his neighbors sometimes. Of course, at the time, I thought you would tell the police yourself—but I understand now that it would have placed you in an—unfavorable light, so I really don't blame you. Still, it is information that the police might..."

"What do you want!" she said hoarsely.

"Want?" Lord, she was beautiful! Her eyes blazed with anger and every inch of her was alive.

"My wants are very simple," I said. "I'm a lonely guy in a strange town. I want a bottle of good wine, a good meal, and a beautiful girl to keep me company—the most natural desires in the world."

She said one word, under her breath, and not a very

nice word at that.

I laughed. "You won't believe this, but I almost never make a good impression on people. That has always seemed unfair, because I'm a lovable guy when you get to know me."

"I'll bet!"

I liked this. I had a feeling that under that mask of hers was something very exciting. Then the cab stopped and I was surprised to see that we were already in the heart of town, at the Lake Hotel.

"Fine!" I paid the driver, assisted her from the cab.

Pat seemed to know her way around so I said, "The choice is up to you. There must be a good saloon somewhere in this place." The decor in the African Room was extremely modern and angular and not much to my taste, but it was better than anything I had seen for five years so I didn't complain.

I looked at Pat when the waiter arrived and she said, "Martini, five-to-one."

I looked at the waiter and he nodded that he had the order. I said, "Bourbon on the rocks," and he went away.

We said nothing until the drinks arrived and the waiter went away again. Then she looked at me, angrily. "Now I want to know the reason for all this!"

"I told you, I was lonely."

"I don't feel like jokes. What is it you want?"

"I told you what I wanted. Maybe it's strange, but it's the truth."

"Understand one thing," she said tightly. "I don't have to stand for this ... this caveman performance of yours. I have friends ..."

"Have you?" I said. "Alex Burton had people in debt to him and might have called them friends, but they don't count now."

Color crept high in her face. "I must have been insane," she said, "when I allowed you to drag me into that taxi. I thought ... I don't know what I thought. But I know one thing, I've had enough." She stood up.

I said, "Sit down!"

She didn't move.

I came half out of my chair. "Listen to me!" I said "You try to leave this room and I'll cause the goddamnedest scene you ever saw! I'll tie you up with the Burton murder and get your name in headlines if I have to print the papers myself! Now sit down!"

She dropped as though she had been shot.

"That's better. Now drink your martini and calm down a little."

She glared at me, then downed the drink angrily. The well-trained waiter was right at my elbow, ready to pick up the empty glass. "Another of the same," I said, "for the lady."

We sat in absolute silence until the drink arrived. I hadn't meant for it to be like this at all, I had meant for it to be a nice, smooth operation carried off in a civilized manner. But, goddamnit, people simply would not allow me to be civilized.

Jesus, I thought, I don't enjoy this sort of thing; I'm no goddamn sadist. A certain amount of violence, sure; like a good fighter, I needed a certain amount of violence to keep my reflexes in condition.

The waiter came and went away again, and still we sat there in silence. But she didn't look quite as angry now. I could almost see her taking control of her emotions, and some of the fire went out of her eyes, and she sat there for a long while, studying me coldly, calmly.

"Well," I said at last, "what do you see?"

"... I'm not sure."

"Believe me," I said, "I didn't enjoy that little scene. I hadn't meant for it to be that way at all. Now, have you calmed down a little?"

"... Yes."

"Fine. Finish your martini, then if you still want to walk out, I won't try to stop you. Is that fair enough?"

"Mr. O'Connor," she said coldly, "I want to ask you once more. What do you want from me?"

I sighed. "I don't know what's wrong here, I honestly don't. We speak the same language, don't we, the American language? I've told you three times, it's a universal plot: boy meets girl, the oldest plot in the world. My methods were unorthodox, I admit it, and perhaps they were all wrong, I admit that too, but believe me, that's all there is to it. To put it bluntly, I saw you, I wanted you, I went after you. Do I make myself clear?"

"Things you want ... Do you always go after them like this?"

"That depends on the situation and the value of the object desired."

"I see." Her hand was perfectly steady as she lifted the martini to her lips. "Do your methods work?" she asked, her gaze lowered.

"Yes," I said, "my methods usually work. Not always, of course; nothing is perfect. But ninety per cent of the time, yes, they work."

"See something you want, take it," she said.

"You amaze me," I said. "Yes, that sums up my philosophy pretty well. It is simple, direct, completely honest."

She lifted her gaze to stare at me. "Honest?"

She was interested now; at least, she was curious, and this pleased me. I said, "Of course. The strong take from the weak. They always have and always shall. That is the first law of Nature, and what could be more honest than Nature?

"That sounds pretty pat for a philosophy."

"Of course it's pat, because it is simple, and honesty is a straight line between the question and the answer."

"It sounds like a negative philosophy, at the very least."

"Negative? That depends on one's definition of good

and evil. But first philosophy itself must be defined. 'Philosophy,' said a certain Frenchman, 'is the pursuit of pleasure.' What could be more sensible? Now, how do you achieve this philosophic pleasure? Pleasure is brought about through the fulfillment of personal ambition, the acquisition of wealth or power, or the titillation of our senses and appetites."

She sat there for a moment, still staring very soberly at my face. "I'm sorry," I said. "I don't mean to bore you."

"... I'm not exactly bored," she said, after a moment. "I have a question."

"Shoot."

"Who is the Frenchman you admire so much and love to quote?"

I laughed. "I was afraid you would ask that—please don't allow his reputation to obscure his logic. His name was the Marquis de Sade."

"Where did he die, this hero of yours, this Marquis de Sade?"

"... In a madhouse, I believe."

She smiled thinly. "That's some philosophy you've adopted, Mr. O'Connor!"

I could have carried my argument forward and perhaps made a point or two, but I was no longer interested in abstract criminal theory. It had served its purpose for the present, it had got Pat Kelso curious as to just what the hell kind of guy I was, anyway.

Then she jarred me. "I met a man once," she said, "who had ideas much the same as yours. His name was Venci. John Venci, I believe."

"Venci?"

How much did she know? How much was she guessing? I said, "I don't believe I know the name. Who is he?"

"He is dead," she said flatly. "He was a gangster and very powerful, but now he is dead."

"... I see." Then I said, "I find this interesting—you and

a gangster, I mean. You don't seem to go together. How did you meet?"

"Through a ... friend."

"Alex Burton?"

That was the sensitive nerve. Something happened to her, especially to her eyes, when his name was mentioned. I said, "All right, it isn't important, we'll forget it." I noticed that her glass was empty again, and I remembered that I had made a promise and would have to keep it. Pat Kelso was no person to be held by chains alone; there had to be something stronger than that: curiosity, hate, fear. But some attraction had to be there, and it had to be a good deal stronger than mere intimidation. There came a time, after the first show of force, when a trainer had to take a dog off a leash and see if he would heel of his own accord.

The waiter was there again, ready to pick up the glass. I said, "It's up to you. Do you still want to go home?" For a moment I thought she was going to say yes. She glanced at me, surprised at first, then suddenly she amazed me by laughing. "I don't think I ever saw a man so sure of himself!"

"Does that mean you'll have dinner with me?"

"... Yes. I believe it does."

I felt like a million dollars. I was beginning to live, actually beginning to enjoy myself for the first time since I crashed off that prison work gang. We left the Lake Hotel and went to a place called *Morani's*, an old Colonial mansion—rather, what *looked like* an old Colonial mansion. The owner himself hustled forward when he saw who we were, looking mildly shocked and grieved, and I guessed that this was one of the places that Burton and Pat had favored while Burton had still been alive. This suited me fine; it amused me to walk in and take over where the late ex-governor had left off, right down to his girl and favorite restaurant.

"Miss Kelso," the owner said gravely, "I cannot tell you how very pleased to ..."

"To see me back again?" Pat laughed and patted his hand. "Angelo, you know I could not live in Lake City and not visit the famous *Morani!* Angelo, this is Mr. O'Connor, an old friend, and we are starved. Do be a dear, will you, and tell Mario we are here."

Angelo Morani shook my hand, but his heart wasn't in it. After we were seated I said, "Who's Mario?"

"The chef, of course."

"Oh, I see. The minute we come in the chef drops everything and takes our order personally. Who are we supposed to be, anyway, visiting royalty?"

She smiled. "They remember me as Alex Burton's ... friend. I'm not kidding myself; the reflected glory won't last long, but as long as it does last I can't see why I shouldn't take advantage of it, do you?"

For just a moment I reached across the table and took her hand. "You're quite a riddle," I said. "A few minutes ago you turned pale every time I mentioned Burton, now you're taking it in stride."

"Maybe I've come, at last, to join the Living, as you advised."

"You won't be sorry. Burton had his day in this town, but, believe me, I'll have mine too. And soon. Pat, I'm going to let you in on a little secret. I'm going to turn this town upside down and shake it till its teeth rattle—so help me, within a few months nobody'll remember Alex Burton ever lived!"

She looked at me, steadily. "When you say it like that, I can almost believe you will do it."

"I'll do it, all right. I'll ..."

I looked up and the chef, a great, red-faced man with bristling mustaches and lively eyes, stood beaming down on Pat.

"Miss Kelso!"

"Mario, it's wonderful to see you again!"

"Thank you!" he said, obviously not annoyed at being called from his kitchen. "Now!" he beamed. "For dinner, what shall it be? But wait, let Mario do it! A great surprise, what do you say to that?"

"I think it's wonderful. You do that, Mario, a surprise for two."

I said, "Tell me something." And she looked straight through me, waiting. "Tell me," I said, "why you decided not to walk out on me."

"Credit it to momentary insanity."

I laughed. "All right, now tell me something else, about you, Pat Kelso."

A full minute went by before she said a thing. Then, at last, when she did speak, her voice was surprisingly calm and pleasant. "There isn't much to tell; my family was poor but proud, as they say. My father sent me to the best schools, although it plunged him into bankruptcy, and I failed to live up to his expectations by marrying well-to-do, so ... I began looking for a job."

"That's how you met Burton?"

"... Yes."

"One thing I would like to know. Were you in love with him?"

I thought she wasn't going to answer at all this time. But finally she looked at me with a forthrightness that was stunning. "I'll say this one time, just one time, and then we'll never speak of Alex Burton again."

"That's fair enough."

"No, I don't think I loved him," she said flatly. "But I adored him. He was the kindest, gentlest, most generous man I have ever known. When I was with him he made me feel that I belonged to another world. The world my family had once belonged to, long ago."

That stopped me for a moment. I had only to look in

her eyes to know that she actually believed it, what she had said about Burton.

Great God! I thought, what a politician he must have been! That thieving bastard, that robber of the poor, that murderer who could look a girl like Pat in the eye and convince her that he was kind, gentle, generous—a saint, practically! I felt the laughter bubbling in my throat but didn't dare let it come out. What a joke this was!

But she would never know. Not from me. I had the good sense to see that nothing I could say would change it—it would only make her hate me—so I said nothing. I accepted it.

After all, what difference did it make now? Alex Burton was dead.

Then I began getting a hunch about Pat Kelso. I began to wonder if it had been Burton's gentleness, kindness, that had really drawn her to him. I wondered if it couldn't have been his "generosity" that had really hooked her ...

I saw the wine waiter headed in our direction and I said quickly, "I told you once I was going to shake this town till its teeth rattled. And I will. A lot of loose change is going to fall from a lot of pockets—how'd you like to be standing in just the right place to catch some of it?"

She smiled, mostly with her eyes.

"You amaze me, Mr. O'Connor. I'd like very much to be standing there when the money starts to fall."

CHAPTER ELEVEN

It was called the Marlow Building, a relatively new and modern building in downtown Lake City. I walked in and studied the building directory for a moment, then headed for the elevator. The elevator starter, a uniformed girl of about twenty-four, held the car when she saw me coming.

"Going up, sir?"

"I sure am!"

Yes sir, there was no doubt about it. I was on my way and the sky was the limit. The elevator doors came together with a whisper, shutting out the marble-floored lobby, the small exclusive shops. It's quite a building, all right, I thought, and it must cost Parker King a pretty penny to keep a suite of offices in it. A man with a very tall stack of blue chips. That was Mr. King, Senator Parker Everest King.

I felt nine feet tall when I stepped out of the elevator on the fourteenth floor. This was one of those buildings that had no thirteenth floor—ten, eleven, twelve, fourteen. But it was still the thirteenth floor, no matter what they called it, and Parker King was going to find it plenty unlucky; you could bet your life on that.

I walked left from the elevator and there were eight doors, all in a line, all with frosted glass panels, all with the lettering on them: THE P. E. KING COMPANY CONTRACTORS. I opened the first door and went in.

The receptionist, an attractive, businesslike woman of about forty-two or -three, said, "May I help you, sir?"

"Yes, I'd like to see Mr. King."

"I see. Mr. King has a very full morning, sir, I'm afraid I couldn't possibly disturb him just now. May I have your name, sir, and the nature of your business?"

"William O'Connor, which won't mean anything to him. The business is ... confidential."

"I see," she said, writing it down: William O'Connor, no appointment, confidential business. She took the note and went into another office.

She returned. "I'm sorry, Mr. O'Connor, but Mr. King's morning schedule is completely filled. Perhaps if you could come again tomorrow, or call ..."

"I'm afraid that will be impossible," I said.

I took an envelope from my inside coat pocket, selected

one of several photostats that had been in it, and put the other photostats back in my pocket. I borrowed the receptionist's fountain pen and wrote across the face of the photostat: *This will give you an idea how confidential my business is. O'Connor.*

I said, "Will you please give this to Mr. King?"

She didn't like the idea of disturbing the Great Man again, but that hocus-pocus with the photostat had looked pretty important and she didn't want to miss any bets. The receptionist gave the envelope to the other girl, and the girl took it into the other office, and after a moment she came back, spoke to the receptionist, both of them looking at me.

"Mr. King will see you, Mr. O'Connor," the receptionist said.

"Thank you."

"This way, sir," the other girl, the secretary, said.

I followed her out of the front office, through the other office, and through the doors of the sanctum sanctorum itself.

Parker King was waiting, and he was angry. He stuck the opened envelope under my nose and said, "What the hell's the meaning of this!"

"I thought it was perfectly obvious." I said. "It's blackmail."

That stopped him. He was a good looking guy about forty, well tanned, well dressed, well fed, and no doubt well satisfied, until I had stepped in with that photostat and knocked the wind out of him. There is some sort of perversity in most humans that makes it impossible for them to call a spade a spade, no matter how obvious it is.

"Blackmail," I said. "There's no use chasing our tails and wasting time. You have in your hand a photostatic copy of some very important and confidential documents, made from originals which are in my possession, though not on my person, naturally. To get down to cases, you will notice that there is a cancelled check, made out to cash and signed by you, in the amount of thirty-five hundred dollars. And here is a photostat of the county commissioner's bank statement —please note the deposit date of May Third, the day after you wrote the check; the entry is a deposit of thirty-five hundred dollars. Strangely enough, here is a photostat from the commissioner's office records which shows that your firm was awarded a large turnpike construction contract on the very day the check was written, despite the fact that there were seven bids lower than the one your firm submitted.

"How am I doing, Mr. King? Is the picture beginning to form? Well, I'm not through yet, there's still the clincher, there's the photostat of a memo you made dated May First—can you read it, Mr. King? You're damn right you can. It says, 'See Anderson 11 A.M. 5-3 re turnpike deal'. It's a note made in your own hand, on the memo pad that's on your desk right now. Well, King, how does it look? Have I got you or haven't I?"

He looked gutshot and sick, but there was still some fight in him. "You punk," he said hoarsely, "Do you know who you're talking to! Do you know what the penalty for blackmail is in this state!"

I knew who I was talking to, all right. I took a step forward and pushed him against his desk. "Do I know who I'm talking to?" I said. "Now there's an idiotic question— I know more about you than your own mother could ever guess. I know you for the thieving sonofabitch you really are, King, and that's not just guessing; I've got the proof. Sure, you're a state senator, which bothers me not at all. You're a state senator who has a pretty good chance of becoming Governor someday, if you keep your nose clean, and that's exactly the reason you're going to do as I say, because you want to be Governor, and because you haven't got the guts to do anything else. Oh, I know who I'm talking to, all right. You think I'd be damn fool enough to approach someone with a deal like this unless I knew him?"

I let him go and he almost fell.

"What ... what do you want!"

"Money, of course."

"And what ... do I get for it?"

"I am not an unreasonable man, Mr. King. Get in and get out, that's my motto. I'm here to sell you the originals of those photostatic copies you have in your hand—my price is twenty thousand dollars."

"What!"

"Twenty thousand dollars," I said. "Think of it, that's not so expensive for complete protection. You'll be buying the original documents, remember that, not the copies. You won't have to worry about my milking you year after year. One price buys everything, a clean bill of health. Anyway, what are you hollering about? You made more than twenty thousand out of that contract deal with Commissioner Anderson."

His face was gray. "I won't pay it!"

This was just reflex. His morale had taken a beating and he had to make a show of resistance for his own benefit.

"All right," I said.

That surprised him.

"What?"

"I said all right, I can't force you to buy something you don't want. All I can do is take the documents to the proper authorities and see that they get the proper publicity. You know, maybe I had you figured wrong, King. I figured your political life was worth at least twenty thousand; I had it figured all along that you would consider it a bargain at that price. Well, I guess I was wrong."

He looked a hundred years old. "... Ten thousand," he said finally.

I hooked a chair with my foot, pulled it up and sat

down. "I have nothing important to do," I said. "I can wait. If you want to play it cute, it's all right with me."

He put his hands to his face and for one horrible moment I was afraid he was going to cry. But he got hold of himself. He wiped his forehead with a crisp white linen handkerchief, then tucked the handkerchief back into his chest pocket, very neatly.

It didn't take long. "... All right. Twenty thousand. Now where are the originals?"

This was more like it. "I told you I didn't have them on me. But I'll have them this afternoon, say one o'clock."

He nodded heavily.

"At the Central Bus Station," I said. "I'll have the papers and you have the money, in small bills, nothing over a twenty. One o'clock will give you plenty of time to arrange it at the bank."

I stood up, smiled. "Mr. King, it's been a great pleasure to do business with a man of your intelligence."

The girl in the second office, the secretary, smiled as I came out of King's office. "It's a beautiful day, isn't it, sir?" she said.

"It sure is that! It's a beautiful day!"

But it was only the beginning. Let's see now, I thought, floating down the corridor toward the elevators. Let's see, King buys one bill of goods for twenty thousand, and there must be at least enough material in his files for four more sales. Four times twenty thousand ... five times twenty thousand, counting the present deal, came to an even hundred thousand. One hundred thousand beautiful dollars, that's what Parker King was worth to me if I handled it right! If I didn't push him too hard or too fast. *One hundred thousand dollars!*

Still, that was only the beginning!

In John Venci's strongbox there were at least fifteen names that should be worth plenty. Conservatively, there were at least ten names that should be worth as much as

King. But let's be super-conservative, let's say they're worth only half as much as King ... let's see, that would be *five times one hundred thousand dollars*, that was what John Venci's strongbox was worth to me!

And this was the kind of money that John Venci had passed up for the sake of revenge! With Venci it figured. He'd had all the money he could use; he could afford to be a theorist. A man like that could afford to kick a million bucks in the face if he felt like it, but not me.

Not Roy Surratt.

No sir, there was a time to be practical, and this was it. After I had milked this thing for all it was worth, maybe I too could afford to retire to a private monastery and contemplate the philosophic truths of crime. But not now. By God, I was just beginning to live, and I was going to enjoy it!

CHAPTER TWELVE

At exactly one o'clock Parker King walked into the Central Bus Station. His face was mask-like, his eyes tired and expressionless. He carried a thick leather briefcase and looked more like a European diplomat headed for the United Nations Assembly than a state senator on his way to pay twenty thousand dollars worth of blackmail.

I was at the lunch counter having a sandwich when he came in.

He looked like he needed a sandwich. And plenty of milk and sun and lots of rest. Parker King looked like a man who was very close to a nervous breakdown.

"The papers," he said huskily. "For God's sake, if anyone should see me here, that alone would be enough to make them suspect something. A bus station!"

I took the papers from my inside coat pocket and gave them to him. Nervously, he glanced at them, then sagged with relief when he saw that everything was there. "There's just one thing," he said. "I don't want to see you again, ever, understand?"

"I understand."

He sat the briefcase down and started to go, and I said, "Just a minute, I'll go outside with you and carry the briefcase. You had it in your hand when you came in. We don't want somebody to think you forgot your briefcase and I was trying to get away with it, do you?"

"I ... hadn't thought of that."

"You should set aside an hour every day," I said, "just for thinking. You'd be surprised how much trouble you can avoid through a little thinking. Well, I'm ready."

I picked up the briefcase and we went out together, as though we were buddies, or anyway business acquaintances. When we got to the sidewalk I said, "I don't suppose I need to ask what's in this briefcase."

He looked at me, hard, then turned and motioned to a taxi starter. I grinned. Yes sir, this had been a hell of a day!

At five o'clock that afternoon I was back in front of the Burton Manufacturing and Construction Company watching the flow of white-collar workers as they crowded out of the building. I called out when I saw Pat.

Her eyes widened when she saw the car. It was a Lincoln, just like the one Dorris Venci had, only this one was black and brand new. She crossed through a line of waiting taxis to where I was parked.

"Where on earth did you get that?"

"Just drove it off the show room floor. Get in."

"Well...." She shook her head, surprise still in her eyes. I got out then, went around the car and opened the door for her. She turned and stepped inside. After I went around and got under the wheel again, she said, "Are you sure you just drove this off the floor?"

"Look at the indicated mileage; exactly twenty-seven miles. What do you think I did, steal it?"

"I must admit the possibility crossed my mind."

"I can afford an automobile like this. Remember what I said last night about turning this town upside down and shaking it?"

"... Yes."

"And you said you'd like to be standing in the right place when the money started to fall?"

"I ... might have said something to that effect; I can't be sure."

"You can be sure about one thing," I said. "Look in the back seat."

She turned her head and made a small sound when she saw the package. It was a hell of a fancy package, a big flat box wrapped in black and silver striped paper, tied with a black and silver ribbon.

"What is it?"

"It's for you," I said. "This is the day money started to fall, and you were standing in the right place."

She didn't touch the package; she was still a little stunned, and that amused me. "I think I called you a peasant last night," she said after a moment. "It looks as though I'll have to take back those words."

I grinned. "You want to open it now, or wait?"

"Where are we going?"

"To my apartment," I said. "This is a day worth remembering, this is a day to celebrate. I bought some wine, and had a caterer get the place in shape and prepare some snacks. How does it sound?"

"... Interesting. Unusual, I must say, but interesting."

"We'll wait, then, with the package. All right?" She nodded, and I switched on the Lincoln and moved it through the crowded traffic. We had traveled six or seven blocks and she hadn't said a word.

Then: "I don't suppose you want to tell me where your

sudden riches came from ... I know it's none of my business."

"It's simple. I had something to sell and found a man who wanted to buy; the very soul of commerce, the life blood of capitalism, the age-old law of supply and demand. Look," I said, "I got off on the wrong foot with you; I admit it. I got a little rough, but actually I'm not a rough guy at all. Believe me, everything is fine."

"Forget it."

I parked the Lincoln in one of the garages behind the apartment building and Pat and I used the rear entrance to get to my place. I had the package under my arm, anxious to see her face when she opened it. *This will thaw her out*, I thought. *If she doesn't react positively to the stimulus of this package, then I've wasted a hell of a lot of time studying the science of human motivation!*

"Here we are," I said, putting the key in the lock. I had opened the door, just a little, just a crack, when I saw Dorris Venci there in my apartment! I had just started to shove the door all the way open and step inside for Pat to enter, when I saw her sitting there, motionless, those Zeiss-lens eyes focused emptily on my face. I closed the door, fast.

"Look," I said, "I just happened to think of something. Something I forgot to do. Will you do me a favor, will you go in your own apartment for a few minutes, powder your nose or something, until I get everything just right? I don't know about you, but this is a big day for me, and I want to be absolutely sure that everything is right. Will you humor me?"

An eyebrow lifted the slightest bit, that was all. "Of course," she said.

She gave me her key and I opened the door to her own apartment. "Just a few minutes," I said heartily, "this isn't going to take long."

Alone, I stood there in the hallway thinking: Christ, I

hope she didn't see Dorris in there! She would recognize her sure as hell and pretty soon she would start putting things together. Pat Kelso was no dummy. She wasn't just another piece of gorgeous sex machinery; she had a brain.

I took a deep breath, feeling the anger flow over me, feeling it in my guts, in my muscles, in my brain. I gave myself a few seconds to calm down, then shoved the door open and went in.

I had forgotten about the caterer. She was a short, fat German woman of about fifty, very neat and businesslike in a starched white dress, gleaming white shoes, a small heart-shaped light blue apron. She looked perfectly anti-septic and sterile and happy.

"Oh, Mr. O'Connor," she beamed, "I believe everything is in order. Everything, just as you ordered it. Smoked turkey, baked ham, a shrimp bowl, mushroom salad. The sweetbreads are in the chafing dish, sir, over the warmer, and the wine is in the refrigerator ready to be iced."

"Thank you," I said, "everything looks fine." Dorris Venci sat as though she were hypnotized, saying nothing. I paid the woman from the caterer's, made a deposit on the dishes and told her she could go.

I turned to Dorris and said, "I'm getting pretty goddamn tired of your walking into my place like this. To be per-fectly honest, I'm getting tired of you. Can't you see I had something of my own arranged here?"

She turned those eyes on me, and only then did I see how washed out she looked. Her face had aged ten years in the past two weeks.

"You ... haven't called," she said flatly. "I ... haven't heard from you in several days."

"Listen to me," I said, "we'd better get something straight, and right now. You have no hold on me at all; the minute you turned over your husband's strongbox, it was over. You didn't buy a damn thing. Is that clear?"

Suddenly she put her hands to her face, covering her

face.

"Now what's wrong with you?"

"I wish I were dead!" Her voice came muffled through her hands. "I wish I had the courage to end it!"

"Great God!" I groaned, "don't go into that act. I couldn't stomach it. Look here, you're a good-looking woman, there are plenty of men who would go for you in a big way. Stop seeing yourself as so damned abnormal. You know what's really wrong with you? Not your abnormality, but your fear of it. You're a starving woman, surrounded with food, and you haven't got the guts to admit you're hungry. You can't go on pretending that your husband *took advantage* of you, or that I did. You wanted it, and you know you did, desperately."

"No!" It was almost like a small scream.

"Then why did you come here?"

"I ... I love you...."

I laughed. "That's what I thought you would say. You don't love me, but you do need me. Or think you do. Just the way you needed John Venci. He was the only man in the world for you, almost a god, simply because he knew about you, and you didn't have to tell him. As long as you didn't have to admit it to yourself, you could go on pretending that you were normal, whatever that means.

"Well," I said, "I'm going to tell you one more thing. You're going to wind up in a nuthouse, and soon, if you don't snap out of it. You don't have your husband now. And you don't have me, either, because I'm tired of you. What you ought to do is go down to the docks and pick up a gorilla that would really know how to treat you."

"No!"

"All right. If you'd rather have the nuthouse."

She took her hands from her face and sat there shuddering. She was looking into the future and seeing nothing but darkness. "Well," I said, "I tried to tell you, but you won't listen. Now you've got to get out of here."

"... Roy." It was barely a whisper. "Please ... don't send me away!"

"I told you I'm through with you. I told you what's wrong with you and what you need to set you right. That's all I can do."

I took her arm and pulled her out of the chair. I guided her to the door, made sure that the hallway was clear and shoved her out.

I was through with Dorris Venci.

I've made that clear, I thought, even to her. I'm through with her. If she wants to kill herself, that's fine with me. If she winds up in a nuthouse, that's fine too, I just don't give a damn what happens to her. But she had better keep away from me!

I got myself calmed down, finally. I went to the bathroom and rinsed my face with cold water and felt a little better. Crazy damn woman!

CHAPTER THIRTEEN

"How do you like it?"

"It's beautiful! It's positively beautiful!"

"Come on in the bedroom and look at yourself in the mirror."

"Really, you shouldn't have done this! It's much too expensive!"

"That's nonsense. All good things come expensive, I learned that long ago, while dishwashing my way through college."

It really was a hell of a coat. To be perfectly truthful, it was much more coat than I had figured on at first, but the minute I saw it I knew that nothing else would do. It was a French import, a Balmain, with an exterior of oyster white nylon velvet which is absolutely the most decadent material ever created by the hand of man, and it was completely lined with natural wild mink. The fantastic extravagance of lining a coat with wild mink had completely fascinated the more bizarre aspect of my nature. When they first showed it to me I had burst into laughter. How many Frenchmen would go without shoes this winter, how many Parisian bellies would be empty—and who gave a damn? "That coat," I had told the sales girl, "is absolutely the goddamnedest, most decadent example of a completely lost civilization that I have ever seen—and I'll take it!"

Pat hugged the coat around her and studied herself from all angles in the bedroom mirror. She had the kind of poise that could not be taught, it was the result of a long purebred bloodline and nothing else. She was class, every inch of her, and that coat was just for her.

"It comes off pretty well," I said. "If there are any changes you want on it, the shop it came from will take care of it."

"I wouldn't have it touched!" she said. "Not for anything in the world! It's just perfect ... but it frightens me when I think what it must have cost!"

It had cost damn near as much as the Lincoln, but it was worth it, every penny. I said, "From now on we don't consider price tags, we don't even look at them. Now how about some wine?"

"... All right."

She kept posing, turning, staring at herself in the mirror. Strangely, she hadn't smiled, not once. From the time she opened the package she had registered a good many emotions, but she hadn't smiled. She had wrapped the coat around her, tightly, hugged herself in it, almost as though she were trying to lose herself in the sheer luxury of it. There was a bright ecstasy in her eyes as she burrowed deeper and deeper into the incredible softness of the fur, and for a moment I imagined that she was trying to hide, that she was receding into the soft, secure folds of fur.

I had learned some things about Pat Kelso, and I understood a little of what she must have felt at that moment. At one time the Kelsos had had everything. They were an old family, and very proud, but unfortunately the ability to make money had not grown with their great pride. Pat's father had been forced into bankruptcy, and later, suicide. It must have been quite a comedown for this girl of beauty and breeding. And I could appreciate how she must have felt, smothering herself in a four thousand dollar Paris coat, returning to the past for a moment, in that symbol of lost glory.

I understood. I was pleased.

I had found her Achilles heel, as I had found Dorris Venci's. Now I knew to what frequency Pat Kelso vibrated, and I could control her as surely as an audio oscillator could control the wave form in an amplifier.

Yes sir, I thought, in this world a man must be audacious. With audacity and brains, there's nothing a man cannot do.

Nothing!

"This is absolutely the most beautiful coat I ever saw!" she said.

"If you can tear yourself away from that mirror for a minute we'll get on with the serious business of tasting the wine."

"What wine can possibly be as important as this beautiful coat!"

"This wine. I went to a lot of trouble finding it, and there are damn few bottles left in the world."

She glanced around as I broke the wires on the neck and very gently began nudging the cork back and forth to loosen it. When it came out with the familiar pop, she said, "Oh. Champagne."

"My dear lady, it's more than Champagne, much more than that. It's a life blood, it's the very last of the truly great Ambonnay's."

Age had robbed the wine of nothing, which is more of a rarity than the casual wine sipper might think. It hit the bottom of the glass with plenty of life, its wonderful bouquet as delicate as moonlight. I handed a half-filled tulip glass to Pat and she sipped, still trying to sneak glances at the mirror.

"Ummm. Good."

"Good!" I was actually becoming impatient with her. "If you were anybody else," I said, "anybody else in the world, and I had just handed you a glass of this nectar and you had taken a distracted sip and mumbled 'ummm, good' do you know what I would do?"

"That's a bit involved, but what would you do?"

"I would throw you the hell out of my apartment?"

"But only if I were anybody else in the world?"

"Yes."

"Then I needn't worry." And she smiled, strangely. But it was the first smile of the day and my impatience dissolved. "Okay," I grinned, "the wine is ummm, good, and if you'd like to swig it from the neck of the bottle, that's all right with me. This is no day to get bogged down in a lousy bottle of wine."

I was in a rosy mood again. There's nothing like a really significant conquest to put spice and zest in this business of living.

I said, "How about some food? I'll put a plate together for you and you can get it in front of the mirror."

She laughed softly. "Thank you just the same. But a girl simply doesn't fall heir to a coat like this every day of her life. I'm much too excited for food ... do you mind?"

"Not at all. This is my day not to mind anything, this is my day to indulge in sweetness and light, even if it chokes me. But I do get hungry once in a while. It's the peasant in me, no doubt."

She laughed again, and it was a fine sound. Nodding at the table, she said, "Please don't let me stop you."

"From this day forward nothing will ever stop me."

I helped myself to the iced shrimp and Russian dressing. Then some white meat topped with a thin slice of ham; and finally some hot sweetbreads. Pat simply couldn't stay away from that mirror.

I laughed and she looked around.

"What's the matter?"

"Nothing. Not a thing in the world!"

"You're awfully satisfied with yourself today, aren't you?"

"I sure am," I said. "It's been a wonderful day, and it's only beginning." When I finished eating I went into the kitchen and iced down another bottle of wine. She had finally torn herself away from the mirror.

"Don't you want to tell me about it, this wonderful day of yours?"

"Some other time," I said, "but not today." I refilled the glasses from the new bottle and she sat beside me on the couch. Every so often when I was near her it would hit me, and it hit me now ... I looked at her and felt my insides go to buttermilk. Great God, I thought, she's beautiful.

She sat there looking at me, very seriously now; then suddenly she surprised me by smiling. "What is it?" I said.

"It just occurred to me that I know absolutely nothing about you. I don't even know what you are called—is it William, or Will, or Bill ..."

"It's Roy," I said without thinking, forgetting for a moment that Dorris Venci had changed my name for me. Then I remembered and said, "It's what my mother used to call me."

"Roy," she smiled. "Roy, and your name is William O'-Connor. Well, I suppose that's consistent enough, for you."

"The explanation would bore you," I said.

"But what about *you?*" she said, almost absently, as

though she wasn't really interested at all but considered it polite to ask. "You must have a history of some kind, a background, a past. Or would that bore me, too?"

"Probably," I said. "I started with an empty belly and a high intelligence quotient, and now I don't have the empty belly."

She smiled, faintly. "Isn't that over simplifying it just a bit?"

"This is a pretty simple world when you get right down to it. When I was a kid I learned to grab fast when we were lucky enough to have food on the table. It took me several years to realize that everyone was grabbing for something, always, and the only trick in getting what you wanted was in grabbing just a little faster than the others."

"And that is the rule you live by?"

"That is my rule."

I guess she knew it was going to happen, from the way I was staring at her. After all, you don't give a girl a coat like the one I had given her just because you liked the way she set her hair. I made a grab for her but she already had her guard up and had pushed herself down to the other end of the couch. She tried to get up but I grabbed again and this time I got her.

I was amazed at the strength in those smooth, firm arms of hers. She didn't make a sound; there was no hint of panic in her eyes, but I had a hell of a time pulling her down with me just the same. But I did it, finally. I got her shoulders pinned against the back of the couch, I threw my weight against her and got both her arms in my hands and she was completely helpless. She knew she was helpless and stopped the fight.

She looked at me with perfect calm. "... Now what?" she said.

"See something you want, grab it. I told you that was my rule."

"... I see. All right, you've grabbed, now where do you go from here? Really, I'm curious about this rule of yours, I want to know if you can really make it work."

Don't you worry about that, I thought. I'll make it work, all right. Then I forced her head back and mashed my mouth to hers.

It was like kissing a statue, a cold, marble statue. That was one thing I hadn't been prepared for. I'd been prepared for a fight, for a lot of insane gab, for tears, even, but certainly not anything like this. I felt the iciness of that kiss deep in my guts. It made my skin crawl.

I let her go. I couldn't have released her faster if I had suddenly discovered that I *had* been kissing a corpse. That is what it had been like, kissing a corpse.

Then she laughed, softly. "You see, Roy, it's just as I thought. Your rule doesn't always work, does it? Some things you can grab, but woman—they're different. You don't grab women, you draw them to you gently, very gently. And it takes time, too. That's a rule you should adopt; never rush a lady."

For one time in my life I didn't have an answer. I could still taste the iciness of her lips.

She didn't seem to be angry. She seemed more amused than anything. And then she leaned toward me and pressed her mouth on mine, very lightly, and the coldness was gone. She was warm again, and beautiful, and I wanted her like hell. But this time I didn't grab.

"That's better," she said huskily. "That's much better."

I said, "For me this is a new technique. It's going to take some getting used to."

And she smiled.

"You know something?" I said.

"What?"

"You are positively the goddamnedest woman I ever saw, bar none. You change colors faster than a chameleon. Put you in fire and you don't burn."

"I'll take that as a compliment."

I let her enjoy thinking that she was an enigma. But she was no enigma to me. I could open her up and watch the wheels go round. I knew what made her tick; I knew to what frequency she was tuned. All I had to do was look at her in that coat and I knew who was the real boss. It was quite possible that deep in her soul she hated my guts—a possibility that bothered me not at all. I could afford a new Lincoln and a Balmain coat, both the same day—that was the important thing. That was the hook I had in her.

Maybe she was right, maybe grabbing wasn't the best way to get what you wanted every time. Make her come to me, that was the best, the most satisfying answer. And I knew exactly how to go about it. Thanks to my very good friend, Mr. John Venci.

CHAPTER FOURTEEN

His name was Stephen S. Calvart. That was about all I knew about him, except that he was a textbook publisher and had made a considerable fortune by bribing a number of small-time school officials. S. S. Calvart, just a name, the fourth name from the last in John Venci's list of people he didn't like, to be exact, and I had selected it more or less at random out of all the other names.

The Calvart Publishing Company was located on the east side, the seamy side of the city, and the building was a sprawling, crumbling red brick affair that was even more rundown than the neighboring brick heaps that leaned against it.

I parked the Lincoln in the alley behind the building, learned from the elevator operator that the publisher's office was on the fourth and top floor; so that is where I went.

Calvart, it turned out, was an easy man to get to, not at all like King. I smiled at the receptionist, told her that my name was O'Connor, and that I represented the fourth school district and that I wanted to talk to Mr. Calvart about a new edition of history texts for the elementary grades.

That was the magic word: "new edition." In a matter of a few minutes I had progressed all the way to the head man himself. Yes sir, I thought, this is a place that knows how to treat a customer. Walk in and mention a deal and you get the red carpet treatment, no questions asked.

Calvart was on the phone when I came into his office. He waved with a cigar and motioned to a chair. I made myself comfortable and tried to size him up. He was a big man, two hundred pounds at least, and looked more like an ex-hod carrier trying to get used to wearing three hundred dollar suits than a publisher of school textbooks. He didn't look like a man who got where he was by paying scrupulous attention to the rules of the game.

"Now look, Davis," he was saying into the phone, "you've been using that damn elementary social studies three years now. How do you expect kids to keep up with things in this fast movin' world if you handicap them three years right at the beginnin'? What the hell, those texts are outdated and you know it. Now look, I don't want to tell you how to run your business, but I think we'd be smart...." He listened for a minute, then said, "Yeah, all right, but you work on the school boards down there, and the PTA bunch. Sure, Dave, I'll take care of you, don't I always?"

He hung up and turned to me with no change of expression or tone of voice. "O'Connor you say. From the fourth district. I thought Paul Schriver was runnin' things down there."

"Maybe he is," I said. "I don't even know where the fourth district is."

He was vaguely surprised but certainly not shocked. He took a few seconds to relight his dead cigar. His eyes were absolutely expressionless and looked hard enough to cut glass. In all that two hundred and more pounds there was not an ounce of imagination. Facts were his stock in trade, not imagination.

After a moment he said, "I see." And he did see. He had added his facts and knew that I was a man with an angle. "All right, O'Connor, now that you are here, what do you want?"

"Money. Twenty thousand dollars, to be exact, and before you start pushing the button on that intercom box you'd better take a look at what I'm selling."

I pitched a photostat on his desk and Calvart looked at it quietly, still without expression. It was an affidavit, signed and witnessed, concerning a payoff between Calvart and a member of the state school commission, a man by the name of Longly. There was enough dynamite in that single piece of paper to blow Calvart right out of the publishing business for good, and he knew it.

Its effect on him was exactly the opposite of what I had expected. He actually seemed relieved, now that he had all the facts, now that he knew precisely why I had come and what I wanted. He seemed to relax as he studied the photostat, he even smiled, very faintly.

"Very interesting," he said, not looking at me. "Very interesting indeed, if you should also have in your possession the original from which this copy was made."

"I have it, all right, but not in my possession right now."

" ... Your caution is understandable," he said dryly. He began to look pained as he continued to study the document before him. "Sam Longly," he said. "Sam has been my friend for a good many years. Why, I was the one who got him a place on the school commission. It is difficult—extremely difficult to believe that Sam would deliberately destroy himself, and me, in such a manner." Then he looked directly at me. "But the evidence is irrefutable, isn't it, O'Connor?"

"It sure as hell is. Now let's stop this horsing around and get down to business. Is the original of that photostat worth twenty thousand to you or isn't it?"

He closed his eyes for a moment, as though in thought...

"... Yes," he said. "Yes, I'm afraid it is."

"You're sure it is. One book contract can make you another twenty grand and a lot more, but if that paper should get into the wrong hands there would be no more contracts, and you know it."

"Believe me," he said quietly, "I am quite aware of this document's importance to myself, and I have already told you that it is worth twenty thousand dollars to me. However, I do not carry that kind of money with me ... certain arrangements must be made."

This was almost too easy to be real. It was all I could do to keep from grinning—twenty thousand dollars just for the asking! Jesus, I thought, what a hell of a thing this is that John Venci lined up for me!

Now Calvart was studying the tip of his smoldering cigar. "I am not a man to fight the inevitable," he said.

Calvart opened his eyes and looked at me for one long moment with his old hardness. "The details," he said flatly. "I suppose you have them planned."

"Down to the last split second. You'll have the rest of the day to raise the money. Tonight, at eight o'clock exactly, I'll meet you in the Central bus station and we'll make the swap."

He nodded.

I felt like a million dollars. I was half drunk with the excitement and the knowledge of my power, and it was all I could do to keep from laughing right in Stephen S. Calvart's fat face. Yes sir, this was one hell of a world!

I started to get up, but Calvart was up before me, surprisingly fast for a man his size. He came around his desk, and then, without a hint of warning, a ham-sized hand snapped out, grabbed the front of my shirt and jerked me half out of the chair.

"You lissen to me!" he rasped. "You lissen to me, you cheap sonofabitch, and you lissen good!"

I was too startled to make a move. I hung there like some ridiculous scarecrow from the end of his huge arm. I felt an angry heat rush to my face, swell my throat, but there wasn't a thing I could do but hang there. Calvart's self-control had vanished in an explosion of rage. That smooth, professor-like speech of his had suddenly reverted to character.

"You lousy gutter rat!" he grated. "I ought to kill you right here, right where you're sittin', and if you say one word, make one sound, I'll do it! You just lissen to me and get one thing straight; I'm not goin' to be your goddamn patsy, O'Connor. You got me by the tenders this time, but don't think you can keep milkin' me; don't think you can gouge me again; I don't care what you dig up against me. You just keep one thing in mind, O'Connor. You try a thing like this again, and you're dead. I don't care if I burn for it, you're dead!"

Then he let go and I fell back in the chair.

I sat there, every muscle in my body quivering. It had been a long time since a man had talked to Roy Surratt like that—the last one had been Gorgan, the prison guard. And Gorgan was dead. I sat there rigid with anger, feeling rage claw at my guts like a tiger. If I had that .38 I would have killed him on the spot, I would have put three hard ones right in the middle of his fat gut.

But I didn't have the .38 with me and there was nothing I could do. Not now. He simply was too big to handle without a gun, so I had to take it, anything he wanted to dish out. Like he had said, I had him by the tenders, I had him where it hurt, but he couldn't afford to get too damn tough about it as long as I held on.

"All right," he said tightly, in a voice that sounded like it was being squeezed through a needle's eye. "Get out of here."

"… The bus station. You aren't going to forget our date, are you, Mr. Calvart?"

"I won't forget a thing, not a single, goddamn thing, O'Connor, and that is one thing in this world that you can depend on." Then he put his foot on the chair, straightened his leg suddenly, with a kick, and the chair shot half across the room with me in it. "Now get out of my sight," he said hoarsely, "before I really get mad and break your lousy neck!"

I got out. I saw everything through a red haze of rage; my bones felt brittle; my muscles ached; my nerves seemed to lay on the top of my skin. But I got out, somehow. "All right," I kept thinking, "all right you fat sonofabitch, we'll see who's so tough before this day is over!" I walked out of Calvart's office and through the outer offices and past the pale faces and the curious faces of Calvart's underlings, and then I rode the crawling elevator down to the Lincoln. I sat there for a long time.

All I could do was sit there and try not to be sick, try to sweat it out until the poison rage had done its work. I tried to think of Gorgan and the way he had looked when I killed him, and that helped a little, but not much.

I don't know how much time it took, but finally I felt myself begin to relax, my nerves began to settle back beneath the skin, the red rage began to lift.

Maybe another ten minutes passed. I took out my handkerchief, wiped my face, my hands, then I switched on the Lincoln and got out of there.

Stephen S. Calvart's future was settled.

The first thing I did when I got back to the apartment was get the .38. I cleaned it carefully, checked the firing mechanism, oiled it, took the cartridges and wiped them carefully and replaced them.

Then the phone rang. It was Dorris Venci.

"Look, Dorris," I said wearily, "I thought we had an understanding. No more phone calls, no more biology lessons. Now what the hell do I have to do to make you realize that we're through?"

"... Roy!" Her voice had that high pitched twang to it, like a violin string ready to snap. "Roy, I can't take it! I simply can't take it any longer!"

"Oh for Christ's sake!" I groaned.

"Roy, I mean it! I simply can't take it!"

I had no answer. What could you say to a crazy dame like that?

"... Roy!"

"What is it?"

"... Roy, won't you ... I mean, can't I see you, talk to you...."

"Absolutely not," I said, beginning to get mad, beginning to be sorry that our trails had ever crossed. "I told you we were through. I meant it."

There was ringing silence on the line.

"Dorris."

"... Yes."

"Dorris, did you hear me?"

"... Yes, I heard you."

And then she hung up. I stood there with the receiver to my ear, wondering what could be going on in that twisted brain of hers, and finally I shrugged and put the receiver on the hook. She was nuts, just plain nuts, and if I never heard from her again that was going to be fine with me.

The poison of my anger again spread through me like an overflow of adrenalin into my blood stream. I thought: *you better enjoy what's left of this day, Mr. Calvart. You better grab all the throats you want to grab. You better throw all the weight you want to throw, because your time is running out faster than you think.*

But not before I got the twenty thousand.

Pretty soon I'd have the world by the tail; I'd crack it like a muleskinner wielding a snakewhip. I'd wriggle my finger and Pat Kelso would jump through hoops.

That last thought pleased me. She was quite a girl, Pat. She was just the girl for me and no other would do. She would be mine.

I went back to the front room and sat. I held the .38 in my hand and waited. But pretty soon I'd had all the sitting and waiting I could take. There was nothing to do, nowhere to go. Pat was working, and the only other person I knew was Dorris, and I sure didn't want to see her.

At last I did what most lonely and lost people in a strange city do, I went to a movie. It was a double feature and I sat there dumbly, feeling the comfort of the .38 in my waistband and thinking with pleasure how Calvart would look when I pulled it on him.

Maybe this isn't going to be smart, I thought. Maybe I ought to forget my personal feelings and hold the hammer over Calvart for another twenty thousand or so. But the publisher was a tough nut—it would seem that most of Venci's enemies were tough nuts—and there is only one way to handle a tough nut—crack it.

For a while I thought maybe I'd go out and pick Pat up at the factory, but finally I dropped the idea. Don't let it get to be routine, Surratt. Don't let her take you for granted. Let her wonder what's going on for a while, and then knock her eye out with another brand new bankroll. That will bring her around. Yes sir, if I know the first thing about women, that will bring her around, all right.

I killed an hour after the film walking and thumbing through magazines at a news stand, and another hour over dinner, and by that time it was almost eight o'clock. I headed for the bus station.

Calvart was late. I was at the lunch counter having a

cup of coffee and the clock over the ticket windows said five after eight, and still Calvart hadn't showed. But I wasn't worried. He would show. As he had said, I had him by the tenders, and he would come around because there was nothing else for him to do.

It was exactly seven minutes past eight when I saw him. He came in with a group of people unloading from a Chicago bus, looking bigger than life-size, and angry and mean. But he had the money—there was a scarred leather briefcase under his arm—and that was the important thing. I stood up and waved. I thought, start walking, you sonofabitch. This is the last leg of your last mile!

He came over and sat on the stool next to me, putting the briefcase in front of him. "Well," I smiled, "you're a bit late, Mr. Calvart, but I'll forgive you this time."

"It's the last time, O'Connor. You better remember that," he growled.

"Of course, of course."

"Well," he said sharply, "there is an exchange, I believe. Let's get it over with."

"Nothing could be more to my liking, Mr. Calvart." I handed him an envelope. "Here you are, sir, delivered as promised."

He ripped the envelope open and made sure that everything was there. He didn't get up to leave, as I had expected. He sat there glaring at me with those flat, unimaginative eyes. I reached for the briefcase. "It would look better," I said, "if we walked out together."

"All right."

That surprised me too. For a man with his temper, he was taking this mighty coolly. He stood up when I stood up, and we walked away from the counter and through the big waiting room toward the wall of doors. We went through the wall of doors and I imagined that the night air held a smell of electricity, a feel of excitement, but I knew that it was only the excitement and electricity within myself.

This, I thought, is where the fun begins. This is where I show him the gun, this is where I march him across the street to where the Lincoln is parked. Yes sir, I thought, smiling right in his face, this is the beginning of the end, Mr. Calvart!

That was when the man in the bright plaid sports coat stepped up beside me. He was a tall shambling man with a long bony face and a hooked nose. I had never seen him before in my life, but he said, "All right, O'Connor, just take it easy. We're going to walk across the loading ramps, over to that parking lot in the middle of the block, and we're going to do it nice and easy and without any noise, understand?"

His right hand was in his coat pocket. He moved it just enough to let me feel the muzzle of an automatic.

I looked at Calvart and he was smiling.

CHAPTER FIFTEEN

There were people all around us, redcaps, travelers, soldiers, sailors, all of them harried and peevish as they looked for their luggage or the next bus for Dallas, and not one of them as much as glanced at us. I felt a bloody knife of fear twisting in my groin. In a mob like this a man could be shot dead and these stupid cattle would never realize what happened. The man in the sports coat knew it and smiled thinly.

"March, O'Connor!"

I marched. Calvart, who had moved to the other end of the ramp just in case I forced a shooting play on the spot, now ambled toward us at the end of the ramp.

"Everything all right, Max?"

"Everything's fine, Mr. Calvart. He come along nice and peaceful, like a baby. See, he ain't givin' us no trouble at all."

"That's nice," Calvart smiled. "All right, hold him up just a minute and I'll get the Buick."

"What the hell is this?" I said tightly.

"Quiet," Max crooned softly. "Nice and quiet, O'Connor," nudging me in the ribs with the automatic.

"You sonofabitch," I said, "You'll be eating that .45 before this night is over!"

But he only smiled. I was scared and he knew it.

Max and I stayed right where we were and Calvart went on ahead to the parking lot. After a few seconds he came out in a black Buick sedan and pulled up at the curb. I didn't have to have the situation drawn out for me, I knew that I was as good as dead if I ever got into that car. Calvart was a tough boy and sometime during the day he had decided that he wasn't going to pay blackmail, and the only way to stop it was with a bullet.

Good as dead. That dagger of fear kept stabbing in my groin. I had to get to my .38. I somehow had to knock Max's automatic away for a moment, just a moment, and then I would kill the sonofabitch and take care of Calvart later. But how? The muzzle of that .45 was in my ribs, hard and cold, and it didn't waver. I couldn't very well holler cop, even if there had been a cop handy, and Calvart must have guessed that much.

"Start walking," Max said.

This, I thought, is the only chance I'll ever get. I've got to take the chance that Max won't shoot in a situation like this.

But Max was there ahead of me. "Just a minute," he said. Then, with an expert hand, he snapped my .38 from my waistband and slipped it into his left-hand coat pocket, that .45 of his never moving from its position just below my heart. "Now walk," he said.

I walked, feeling the sweat popping out of my face, feeling my knees go to mush, feeling the blossom of fear grow as cold as ice in my stomach. Calvart had the back door open when we got to the Buick. Max shoved me inside. And no one noticed a thing. Out of all those dozens of people milling around the bus station, not a single one of them noticed that a man was being set up for murder right under their noses! Calvart turned around and smiled as Max shoved me over to the far side of the car and then got in beside me. His .45 was out now, in his hand, and it looked ugly and black and as big as a cannon.

"All set, Mr. Calvart. Turn left on Mallart Avenue. Follow it all the way out of town, out by the brickyards. Anywhere out there will do."

"Whatever you say, Max," Calvart said, smiling at me. Then he eased the car into gear, slipping into the stream of southbound traffic.

Jump him, I thought, it's the only chance you have. Somehow you've got to get that .45 away from him while Calvart is busy at the wheel!

I couldn't do it. My guts had gone to buttermilk. I tensed my shoulders, readied for the lunge, but when the time came I simply couldn't force myself to act. I couldn't throw myself into the muzzle of that automatic.

Now or later! I told myself savagely. What's the difference? Calvart's got it planned, he's going to kill you. The least you can do is make a fight of it while you can!

But panic had me in a grip of iron, held me immobilized, helpless, and all I could do was sit there and sweat.

About three blocks from the bus station Calvart turned left on what I guessed was Mallart Avenue. It's a one-way road for me, I thought emptily. I underestimated Calvart ... I made the fatal mistake of underestimating an enemy and for that bit of stupidity I'm going to die. They'll find me tomorrow, or the next day, in some gutter, and the cops will fingerprint the body and identify it as Roy Surratt, and the investigation would stop right there.

That dagger of fear that stabbed in my stomach there began to stir an anger. A great, unreasoning, savage anger, not at Calvart, and certainly not at Max who was just a hired hand brought in for an hour or so to do a job of work. The anger was at myself. You deserve everything you're going to get! I thought savagely. Roy Surratt, criminal philosopher, realistic genius, perfectionist. Well, you slipped, Surratt, and perfectionists don't slip, and because of that little piece of idiocy you're going to get exactly what you deserve; you're going to get a well placed .45 slug in the back of the head; you're going to get your brains spattered all over some lousy brickyard just because you failed, this one time, to scrupulously practice what you preach!

The anger helped some, but not much. I was sick with fear, paralyzed with it, and I began to wish that the mild, cool-eyed killer sitting across from me would go ahead with it and pull the trigger. The waiting was the thing that got me. I was afraid I'd go all to pieces if it lasted much longer. Already my hands were shaking. A small muscle in my throat started to quiver, a nervous ripple flowed over my shoulders and down my back, and a great, yawning emptiness opened in my belly. Great God, I thought helplessly, *I don't want to die! I don't want to die!*

And Max, the hired hand, smiled blandly and held his automatic close to my heart. Calvart slipped the big, quiet car through the streets and the brightness and garishness of the city passed behind us.

At last the pavement ended and the city was just a glare against the low-hanging clouds. There were no buildings at all out here, and very few houses, and the land was also empty, nothing but ragged and torn hills of red clay, brick clay, standing gaunt and almost black in the moonlight. When we came onto the end of the road Calvart braked the Buick and eased onto a deep-rutted, sparsely graveled road, and Max said:

"Anywhere along here will do."

"We'll go on over the next rise," Calvart said.

Max shrugged slightly. A job was a job and he didn't bother himself with the details.

I tried desperately to stop the sickish quivering in my stomach. I tried to pull myself together enough to jump into the muzzle of that .45 ... but I couldn't do it. I simply couldn't force myself to move.

The road was rough and Calvart was taking it easy, crawling along in second gear. Finally we topped a small rise and I could see the squat black forms of the brickyards in the distance.

"Right here," Max said.

"Just a little farther," Calvart said. "There's no use taking chances."

Just a little farther! I knew just how it would happen ... Calvart wouldn't want his car bloodied up if he could help it; they would stop and shove me out, and they would let me run a step or two and Max would apply the careful, gentle trigger squeeze and the door would slam. That would be the end.

The end. I had the horrible feeling that I was going to cry.

That was when Calvart hit the rock.

It was just over the rise and the headlight beams must have shot over it, and I guess that's the reason Calvart didn't see it until it was too late. It was a good sized rock, maybe a foot thick, and maybe it had fallen off a truck or maybe it had just washed loose from the clay embankment and had rolled down onto the road but where it came from isn't important. It was there and that is the important thing.

Calvart hit it with his right front wheel and the Buick lurched suddenly. Max had to make a grab for the back of the front seat to keep from falling to the floorboards, and Calvart himself was cursing and trying to get the car straightened out on the road. Just what I did at that instant is not clear in my mind, but I acted on instinct, I'm sure of that, pure animal instinct, there was nothing planned about it.

The instant the Buick lurched to the left, the instant Max made his grab for the front seat I forgot about my sickness and my fear. I was on Max like a tiger. Grabbing at his gun hand, I drove my knee in his crotch and heard the wind go out of him. I slashed the edge of my hand across Max's wrist and the bone snapped, but a small thing like a broken wrist meant nothing to Max at that moment because he didn't live long enough to suffer from the pain.

I caught the automatic before it hit the floorboards. I jammed the muzzle into Max's throat, into the soft part between the breast bone and the Adam's apple and pulled the trigger.

He never knew what hit him. The slug tore right through his spinal column, almost taking his head off his shoulders.

In the meantime Calvart had to let go of the wheel and had let the Buick go into a ditch and we were stalled. Calvart himself was trying to get over the back of the driver's seat, trying to grab the gun away from me. He never had a chance. I shoved him back against the steering wheel, then got on my knees and shot him three times right in the middle of his fat stomach. He jerked and quivered like some enormous jellyfish, and his mouth flew open, working soundlessly. That was the way *he* died.

I heard a voice saying, "You sonofabitch! You lousy sonofabitch!" I knew it was my voice, but it didn't seem to be coming from my throat, it seemed to be coming from everywhere, and it was high-pitched and taut and almost screaming. At last I jerked the front door open and gave Calvart a shove, and he hit the ground with the mushy sound of an overripe melon.

I was breathing very hard and couldn't seem to get enough air into my lungs. I concentrated for several minutes on pulling myself together and watching the blood soak into the thick floor mat around Max's severed head. Then I got out of the car and began to feel better. Calvart was dead. Max was dead. But I was alive!

I said it aloud. "Alive!" I said it several times, and then I walked around the Buick and looked at Calvart. Only then did I fully realize what had happened, and I felt fine! I felt exactly the way I had the day I killed Gorgan, only better. Much better!

Then I remembered the papers that I'd sold him. I got down in the ditch with him and took them out of his pocket. Then I looked through the briefcase in the front seat and there was nothing in it but bundles of newspaper cut to the size of banknotes, but not even that could smother my elation. Money was the easiest thing in the world to come by, but a man had to stay alive to enjoy it.

That's something you should have thought of, Calvart, before you arranged this little party tonight!

The back seat of the Buick was a mess, and I didn't make it any better by dragging Max out of it. But I had to use the Buick to get back to Lake City and it wouldn't be especially smart to have it loaded down with corpses.

I dumped Max in the ditch on top of Calvart. Tomorrow they would find them, maybe, and there would be a hell of a noise, but there was very little they could do about it. Who would ever tie a thing like this to Roy Surratt?

It occurred to me that I might as well give the police a motive for the murders, any kind of motive except black-mail, so I went back to the ditch and began looking for wallets. This last was a profitable decision, as it turned out. Calvart was carrying almost six hundred, and Max a little over four hundred, probably an advance on the job he was supposed to do. I laughed aloud as I counted it, almost a thousand dollars. Not bad, not bad at all for a night's work, even though it was a little out of my line.

I pocketed the money, took Max's watch and Calvart's watch and diamond ring. No sir, not a bad night's work at all, everything considered!

I switched on the Buick, got it turned around, and headed back toward Lake City.

I parked the Buick on the outskirts of the city and caught a bus downtown. From there I drove the Lincoln to the apartment.

I was over the shakes now. I couldn't imagine how I could have been scared at all. One thing I was sure of— I'd never be scared again. Audacity, Surratt, that's the thing to remember. Audacity and brains—they make a combination that can't be beat!

I felt light headed, almost drunk. I was a giant among men and the twenty thousand dollars I'd lost didn't bother me at all. Money, I reminded myself again, is nothing.

While downtown I had picked up a morning paper, but I hadn't looked at it yet. The Burton killing had slipped out of the headlines, and it was too early for the Calvart murder, so I dropped the folded paper on a table, went to the kitchen and poured myself a glass of milk.

It was still early, no more than ten o'clock. I'd get myself cleaned up. This had been quite a night ... it called for a celebration. So I'd just go over to Pat's apartment....

That was when I saw it. I walked back in the front room and glanced at the paper and there it was—in black headlines just below the fold.

WIFE OF JOHN VENCI FOUND DEAD.
CORONER SAYS SUICIDE

So Dorris had done it.

The first thing I felt was a sense of relief. Well, by God, I thought, I'm glad she had the guts to go through with it. I'm glad to have her off my neck!

She had shot herself, using a little .22 automatic, and it had been a neat, workmanlike job, according to the paper. One bullet in the temple. Well, I thought, that's the end of that. It's just as well that she had ended it this way, for she would have ended up in a nut ward sooner or later if she hadn't.

Then I thought of something that shook me. I thought: Wait a minute, Surratt. Dorris was pretty sore at you this morning when you brushed her off. Could that have had anything to do with her suicide? Could she have been sore enough to have left some incriminating evidence behind?

Jesus! I thought, that's something to think about, all right!

It was possible, I decided, just possible that Dorris had taken this big step *because* of me. If that was the way it had happened, it meant trouble. It very well could mean the end of Roy Surratt! What if she had left a note behind? What if she had talked to somebody—the district attorney, for instance—before taking the bottomless plunge to oblivion?

It shook me. I devoured every word concerning the suicide, and then I went through it again very carefully to see if I could read anything between the lines.

I could find nothing, feel nothing, sense nothing that might implicate me in the affair. It had happened around four in the afternoon, according to the newspaper. The maid was out of the house at the time. Dorris had simply gone to her room, locked herself in and shot herself with that toy automatic. The reporter quoted the maid as saying that Mrs. Venci had not been herself since her husband was killed, and it was implied that grief had been the driving motive behind the act of self-destruction.

It was perfectly simple. The same story about the grief-stricken widow is printed every day, someplace or other.... It is so simple, I thought, that the whole thing stinks. Dorris Venci had been incapable of doing a thing simple and cleanly—I knew that better than any person alive.

Any person alive ...

My experience with Stephen Calvart had made me acutely aware of the importance of staying alive. A man had to use his brain; and that is exactly what I did. If this thing was going to turn out to be more than a simple suicide, I had to know about it, and fast.

The first thing I did was pick up the phone and call Dorris's number. That maid, that sour-faced maid of Dorris's, she was the one who might be able to straighten me out. Finding the maid at the Venci house tonight was a long-shot chance, and this wasn't the night for longshots to come in. I let the phone ring at least a dozen times and finally hung up.

What had been that maid's name, anyway. Ethel? Edith? Ellen? That was it, Ellen, but I had no idea what her last name was or where she might be.

But the police would know. The idea of going to the police for information amused me. I grinned, feeling a bit of the old excitement and elation return as I dialed the operator and got the number.

"Hello," I said soberly, "may I speak to the officer in charge of the Venci case?"

"Who's callin', please?"

"My name is Robert Manley. You see, I just got the news not more than two hours ago, in this evening's paper, the Lake City *Journal-Times*, and I came just as fast as I could, but you see there was some sort of mix-up at the bus station, I missed my connection at Midburg, and that's the reason..."

"Hold on a minute, will you! Now what's this about the Venci case?"

"That's what I was telling you, officer. You see my Aunt Ellen has been in Mrs. Venci's employ all these years and..."

"Will you please try to calm down, sir. Your Aunt Ellen, you said. Do you mean Ellen Foster, the Venci maid?"

"Yes, of course, Aunt Ellen Foster. You see I live in Midberg, and Aunt Ellen is my aunt. My, that is a ridiculous statement, isn't it, officer, but I'm so upset, really, and Aunt Ellen was so devoted to Mrs. Venci ..."

"Please, sir," the voice said wearily, "just what is it you're trying to say?"

"Why I want to know where my Aunt Ellen is, of course! I called the Venci residence, but of course she wasn't there, what with that awful ..."

"All right, all right!" he almost growled. "Just hold on a minute."

I held on, grinning.

"Here it is," he said after a moment. "The investigating officer lists Mrs. Foster's present address as 1214 Stanley Road, a boarding house there, I believe."

"And the phone number, officer. I feel that I simply must call my aunt right away or ..."

"Jackson 4-1952."

"Thank you, officer, thank you very much!"

He groaned and hung up.

Yes sir, if you want information on police matters, then go to the police! Very obliging people, the police. I don't know what I would do without them! Still grinning, I hung up and after a few seconds dialed Jackson 4-1952.

"Hello ..." A toneless voice, peevish and edged with bitterness.

"Mrs. Foster?"

She admitted grudgingly that she was Mrs. Foster and that she had been Mrs. Venci's maid, then I identified myself as Captain Barlow of the police and that didn't do anything to sweeten her mood.

"Sir," she snapped, "I have nothing more to say about that horrible ... accident. I told the police all I know, everything."

"Everything, Mrs. Foster?"

Now her tone was indignant, but she didn't seem to think it strange that a police officer would do his questioning over a telephone, and at this time of night. "Sir," she snapped, biting into the word, "I'm sure I don't know what you mean!"

"No offense at all, Mrs. Foster," I said soothingly, "and we realize that you have been through a lot, the shock and all. Of course we have your statement in our files, but I would appreciate it very much if you would tell it to me again, in your own words."

"Is this absolutely necessary, Captain? Really, I was most thorough in my report to the police a mere few hours ago. Couldn't it wait until tomorrow, at least?"

"I'm afraid not, Mrs. Foster," I said patiently. "This is an imposition on you, we realize it, and that is exactly the reason we decided not to call in person at this hour. I do hope you understand, Mrs. Foster, that police business must necessarily seem rather unusual at times to the citizen, but I assure you ..."

"All right, Captain," she relented. "I have been aroused and awakened, and now please let us be as brief as possible. Actually, I do not see that I can add to my original statement ... however, it was around three this afternoon when Mrs. Venci called me upstairs and asked about the shopping. As it happens, I was just going out to do the day's shopping, but she asked me to wait. She was writing a letter, she said. She wanted to finish the letter and have me mail it on the way to the market."

My heart missed a beat. The news story had not mentioned a letter.

"... Mrs. Foster," I said, "did you mail this letter, as Mrs. Venci asked you to do?"

"Of course. It's all in my original statement."

"Yes," I said, feeling my muscles begin to tighten. "Yes, of course."

"It's rather interesting," she admitted grudgingly, "that you should call at this particular time, Captain. This afternoon your policemen were extremely curious about that letter, although I couldn't imagine why—and still can't, for that matter. They seemed anxious to know to whom the letter was addressed. I tried and tried to remember, but the name simply wouldn't come to me. Then, just as you called, a few moments ago, the strangest thing happened. The name came to me, Captain."

I heard myself saying, "It did, Mrs. Foster?"

"Yes. I remember glancing at the envelope, just to be sure that it was properly addressed for mailing. Keaslo. I feel quite sure that was the name."

It rang no bell. The name of Keaslo meant absolutely nothing to me. I took a long, deep breath. Maybe I was getting myself worked up over nothing. I said, "How about the first name or the address? Do you remember them?"

"No, I'm afraid not, Captain. After all, it was just a glance, a mere precaution."

"I understand, Mrs. Foster. But about the address, was it local or out of town delivery? Can you remember that?"

There was a moment of silence. Then, "Why, I believe it was a local address, one here in Lake City. But of course I can't be certain."

"... Yes." I heard a curious pounding, and then realized that it was my heart knocking against my ribs. "Yes, I understand. Well, probably it means nothing at all, Mrs. Foster. Thank you very much for your co-operation."

"I should have called the police in any event, Captain," she said. "After my remembering the name, I mean."

"Oh, you needn't do that," I said quickly. "After all, I do have the information now, I mean, and ..." I didn't go on. I could feel her hanging there in a sort of thoughtful vacuum. "Mrs. Foster, is something wrong?"

"... No, nothing is wrong, I was just thinking. Captain, I have the feeling that the letter was addressed to a woman. I don't remember the first name at all, but it is my impression that it was a woman's name."

"A woman's name?"

... And then it hit me!

Keaslo. Kelso. They were similar—too much so to bear the weight of mere coincidence. "Mrs. Foster," I said quickly, "I want you to give this serious thought. I want you to test your faculties of recall to the utmost. This woman's name, this name on the letter that you don't remember, was it Patricia?"

There was only an instant's hesitation. "Why, Captain, I do believe it was!"

I covered the mouthpiece and whistled softly. "Thank you, Mrs. Foster, thank you very much!"

"Is that all, Captain?" She sounded disappointed now, as though she wanted to keep talking. But that memory of hers was getting a little *too* good. I wanted it to stop right where it was.

I said, "That is all, Mrs. Foster. Good night." And I hung up.

So Dorris Venci had written a letter to Pat; and then, being assured that the letter would be mailed, she had put a bullet in her temple. An interesting situation, to say the very least.

I dropped to a chair and sat there thinking about it for minutes. A breath of the breeze drifted into the front room and across my face—the night air seemed to hold an exceptional chill for that time of year.

CHAPTER SIXTEEN

Things like this, I thought, are the things that can kill you. But how could I have predicted the actions of an eccentric mind like Dorris's? How could anyone have predicted them? Anybody else, acting on the same impulse, would have mailed the incriminating letter to the district attorney, or the police department, or maybe even to a newspaper or a citizens committee. But not Dorris. Oh no, she had to send the evidence directly to Pat, overlooking the scores of simpler and more direct possibilities.

I wondered about that for a long while. What had been her motive? Jealousy? Hatred? Shame? Probably an equal amount of all three. If her aim had been to destroy me completely she needed only to point a finger of accusation in my direction—the cops would have taken care of the rest. They would have identified me and that would have been the end of Roy Surratt.

It was bad enough as it was. If Pat got hold of that letter I was as good as dead. The way she had felt about Alex Burton, maybe she would try to kill me herself.

And then I relaxed. I could even smile. This, I thought, is where brains and audacity pay off, because Pat will never see the letter. She will never know that I stood behind the gun that fired the bullet that killed her Alex, because I am going to intercept that letter.

I was going to be at the mail box the next morning when the postman arrived, and I was going to get that letter, even if I had to kill somebody else; and that would be the last of my troubles from Dorris Venci.

I felt fine once again. After a moment I picked up the phone and called Pat. The receiver came off the hook almost immediately.

"This is your neighbor," I said.

"Well! I was beginning to wonder if I'd hear from you."

"I've been busy. It's been quite a day—to tell the truth, I'll be just as happy if I never have another one like it."

"It couldn't have been too bad," she said. "You sound pretty pleased with yourself." Then she laughed. "I'll buy you a drink—unless you're still pouting, that is."

"I never pout," I said. "It's stupid. If you don't get what you want the first time around it simply means your technique is all wrong, so you change techniques."

She laughed again and hung up.

When I stepped into her apartment a few minutes later, it hit me all over again. By God, I thought, she's beautiful, truly beautiful!

"I hope you like scotch," she said. "It's all I have."

"Scotch will do."

She was all wrapped up in a pale blue quilted house coat, looking about fifteen years younger than she actually was. She sat on the tweedy couch with her legs folded back, and there was a closed book in her hand and she was smiling.

"Make yourself at home," she said, and then unfolded slowly, lazily, stood up and walked to the kitchen. There was no doubt about it, she was the most beautiful girl I had ever known or seen.

She came out of the kitchen with two drinks in old fashioned glasses.

She laughed and handed me my drink. The book was put back in its place on the bookshelf, and Pat sat beside me on the couch. We sipped our drinks. I didn't care for scotch, but I drank it, trying not to stare at her, reminding myself not to grab.

And I didn't grab. I liked it this way, just the way we were. I liked to hear her talk; I liked just being with her and looking at her. Christ, I thought, I didn't realize how exhausted I really am! This day had drained me completely, emotionally and physically, and all I wanted to do was sit still and let my muscles sag and look at Pat and think of nothing. Nothing important, anyway—such as that letter, or Calvart lying out there in a ditch on the brickyard road.

Then Pat stopped talking and looked at me. "Is there something wrong?" I said.

"No, I was just wondering about you. When you came in you looked so ... vigorous. Now you look a hundred years old."

"Thank you, ma'am, for those kind words."

"You know what I mean," she said. "You look as though you had been fighting the entire world singlehanded."

"Baby, I don't suppose you'll ever know just how good a guess you just made. But it's nothing, really. I'm just beat, that's all."

She let it drop. Not one woman in ten million would have let it drop there, but Pat did. She merely shrugged, and then began talking about the scotch that we were drinking and how long she had had it. I lay back on the couch and smiled at her, and I wanted her more than I had ever wanted any woman in my life, but I didn't touch her, I didn't as much as lift a finger. When she was ready she would let me know.

I turned my thoughts inward as she talked, and I thought what a hell of a pair we could make, Pat and I. Soon I would move out of the lousy apartment building and take her with me, and I would rent the biggest damn suite in the best hotel in Lake City, and we'd start living the way people like us ought to live.

But first she had to come to me. She had to say, "Please take me with you," and then I would take her. All I needed was patience.

She was a queer one, though. She didn't ask questions —not many, anyway. She seemed to have no ambition. She had loved Alex Burton, but she seemed to have forgotten him completely—but, then, it was hard to tell about a woman like her, what she was thinking, what she really wanted. That coat, for instance. She had been as giddy as a bobbysoxer when I had given it to her, but now she seemed to have forgotten that, too.

I don't know just how long I sat there, thinking of nothing in particular, and of everything in general. I thought of all my yesterdays as they might have been; all my tomorrows as I, with my own two hands, my brain and my guts, would make them. Several minutes must have passed before I realized that I was listening to nothing but silence.

I looked at Pat and she suddenly smiled. "You are tired, aren't you? I don't believe you heard a word I've been saying."

"Was it important?"

She laughed softly. "What kind of a question is that? A lady's words are always important. To herself, at least." Then she reached out a hand and touched my hair. I liked that very much. "Perhaps," she said, "you should go to bed and get some sleep."

"I like it here, just the two of us."

"All right. But you must promise to keep up your end of the conversation."

I grinned at her. "That sounds reasonable, shall we discuss religion, politics, or the weather?"

"What's wrong with O'Connor as a subject of conversation? Do you realize that I know absolutely nothing about you, except that you once worked your way through some college or other?"

It was my turn to laugh. "That's a sore spot with me. I just don't like work, I guess."

"... What do you like, Mr. O'Connor?"

That name kept throwing me. I couldn't get used to it—and, too, it reminded me of Dorris Venci who had given the name to me, and thinking of Dorris reminded me of that letter that I had to intercept, and it all got to be a vicious circle, or a net that had fallen around me, and I wondered if I would ever truly get completely out of it.

"What do I like?" I said. "Well, I like you, I think."

"Now there is a left-handed sort of compliment, if I ever heard one!"

"I didn't mean it to be."

"Anyway," she said, "you must like other things. Money, perhaps."

"Money ... of course I like the things that can be done with money, but I don't have much respect for it as such.

Money is the easiest thing in the world to come by, if you know the secret and practice it."

"Well, I am sure that a great many people would love to have the secret. Would you mind telling me what it is?"

"It's all right there in that book," I said, "the one you were reading. Nietzsche proved with crushing finality that the only civilization capable of enduring is one in which the strong are not penalized for taking from the weak. This particular civilization in which we are living calls it robbery, extortion, piracy, and a lot of other things."

She leaned her head to one side, smiling quizzically. "And do you approve of these particular methods of obtaining money?"

"Let us just say that as a philosophy, Nietzsche's can be a very tough one to logically argue down. However, I wasn't going to bring up this subject, was I?"

"You didn't bring it up, I did, and I find it very interesting." She wasn't smiling now, she looked extremely sober. Like a little girl who had just been told that some day she must die. Once again she touched my hair, and I felt the soothing effect of her hand. There was a satisfaction and pleasure in having her reach out, of her own accord, and touch me. This is the way it would be when the time came ... only more so. "Tell me," she said, "what else do you believe?"

"What else do I believe? Well, I believe in strength. And I believe that man should believe in himself."

"You must be terribly bright," she said, in a lighter vein now, smiling. "You must have read a horrible lot of books in order to have developed so many positive opinions."

"As a matter of fact," I said, "you are right. I have read a great many books, during recent years especially. And I have an intelligence quotient of one hundred and forty-nine, which isn't bad when you consider that one hundred and forty-five is usually considered a genius rating."

She laughed suddenly, with surprising merriment. "Coming from anyone else," she said, "such a statement would tag the guy as an insufferable braggart."

"I wasn't bragging, I was merely stating a fact."

"I know," she said, "and that is one of the things about you that amazes me."

"However," I said, "I don't believe that a man of ability should underrate himself."

Once again she laughed. "I can believe that! I certainly can!"

We sat there for quite a long time. And at last she said, "I'm going to have to put you out before long; I'm still a working girl, you know."

I said, "You don't have to be. All you have to do is say the word and you can have anything you want. Anything."

"This is rather unlike you, isn't it? I didn't think you asked for things. I thought you took what you wanted."

"This is my new technique, remember?"

This time she didn't smile. "... Yes. I remember." Then she said, "You frighten me at times ... did you know that?"

"No. I don't mean to. Why do I frighten you?"

"You're so sure of yourself. You have such absolute confidence in your own power to get the things you want."

"That's the way I am; when I say something, I mean it. Remember what I said that night about turning this town upside down and shaking it, and you said you would like to be around when the money started falling?"

"... I was only joking."

"I wasn't joking. Before long I'll hold this town in my own two hands. I'll make it sit up and talk just the way I want it to talk, like a ventriloquist operating a wooden dummy. Don't ask me how I'm going to do it, just believe me when I say it's going to happen."

She looked at me for one long moment. "Yes ... I can

believe you."

"You haven't asked any questions," I said, "and I appreciate that."

"It isn't because I haven't wondered. I wouldn't have been human, not to have wondered."

"But you didn't ask, that's the important thing. That's the way we'll keep it," I took her hand, just her hand and held it. "That coat I gave you," I said. "That was nothing. You can have a closet full of coats exactly like it, if you want them. That Lincoln that surprised you so ... you can have a fleet of them, one for every day in the week, if you feel like it. That is the way I am going to shake this town. That's the way the money is going to fall when I really start moving."

She said nothing, but there was a brightness in her eyes, a strangeness, when I glanced at her and she didn't know that I was looking.

"Think about it," I said.

"... Yes. I'll think about it."

I had her hooked. I could feel it. This was her chance to stop being a working girl and really become somebody. Yes sir, beyond a doubt she was hooked.

Still, it wasn't the time to start grabbing. Instead I let go of her hand and stood up. "See you tomorrow?"

"Yes," she said, "tomorrow."

Let her think it over. Let her dwell on that fleet of Lincolns and that closet full of Balmain coats. I smiled and walked out of the apartment.

CHAPTER SEVENTEEN

That night I slept like the dead.

I awoke slowly the next morning. I lay in bed and let consciousness creep gently, quietly into my brain, and at last I opened my eyes and saw that the sun was high, I had forgotten to draw the blinds and my drab, cramped bedroom was obscenely bright.

The first thing I thought of was Pat. Maybe I had been dreaming about her, I don't remember, but the first thing I thought of was the brightness of her eyes and the way she had looked at me the night before, and I thought pleasantly: Sure as hell, I've got her hooked.

Then I remembered Calvart.

Ah, yes, Mr. Stephen S. Calvart, and a very tough boy he had been, too. But a dead one now. So I forgot about Calvart.

I padded into the bathroom, brushed my teeth, ran some hot water and began to shave. What I needed was some coffee, but there wasn't any coffee in the apartment, and if there had been it wouldn't have done me much good because I made lousy coffee. But all that would be changed before long. Pat would soon be making my coffee in the mornings.

That thought cheered me. I began to whistle as I lathered my face. I had a feeling that this was going to be a fine day, that this was going to be the day the cards started falling on my side of the table. First Burton, and then Calvart, both of them tough boys, but now they were dead and I could forget them. Surely, I told myself, that list of Venci's doesn't contain any more names that would prove as tough as Burton and Calvart. Surely my luck is due to change!

Not until that moment did I remember the letter.

Christ, what time was it anyway? I didn't have a watch,

and there wasn't a clock in the place, but I remembered Pat saying that the postman usually showed up around ten o'clock.

I finished shaving and got out to that mail box as fast as possible. The house porter came around and said it was only after nine and the postman hadn't been around yet. I breathed easier.

It was almost an hour later that the postman finally showed up. From down the hall I heard the familiar rattle of keys the minute he stepped into the building, and I was there at the mail box almost before he was.

"Good morning," I said pleasantly.

"Mornin'," he said, not looking up. He unlocked the boxes, began sorting out a small bundle of letters, dropping the envelopes into the individual slots.

"Name?" he said.

"What?" ... not understanding at first what he meant.

"Your name," he said, still not looking at me, still busy at sorting the envelopes. "You got any mail, you might as well take it now. Before I lock up the boxes."

"Oh, my name's O'Connor, but I'm not expecting any mail. Fact is I'm here to pick up Miss Kelso's mail for her. She asked me to. That's all right, isn't it?"

He shrugged. "Sure, it's all right, I guess, if Miss Kelso had any mail to pick up. But she don't."

I felt my insides shrink. "You must be mistaken," I said, forcing a laugh, forcing myself to remain outwardly calm. "You see Miss Kelso was expecting this letter; she was quite certain that it would be in this morning's mail, and she wanted me to pick it up for her. Maybe you overlooked it."

"Didn't overlook it," he said, completely uninterested. "Everything for this address was in that bundle. Nothin' for Miss Kelso."

My scalp began to prickle. You sonofabitch, I thought

savagely, if you're holding out on me I'll leave you dead right here in the hallway! So help me I'll strangle you if you don't come across with that letter!

He dropped some magazines on the table and began locking the boxes.

I made myself calm down. In spite of his self-assurance he must have overlooked that letter! He *must* have! Then he shouldered his leather mailbag, nodded and started to go. "Please!" I said quickly, licking my lips. "I know this might sound crazy to you, but that letter is very important—to Miss Kelso. You see, well, I promised I'd get it for her, and naturally I don't want to disappoint her. I'd be very grateful if you'd look again, just to be sure. Would you do that, please?"

He said nothing. He went on thumbing through the bundles of envelopes, and I felt a sick emptiness in the pit of my stomach as bundle after bundle was dropped back into the bottom of the bag.

"Isn't it there?" I asked. "It's there somewhere, isn't it? It got misplaced?"

He finished with another bundle, the last one, and once again shouldered the bag. "Nope. Just like I told you the first time, there's nothin' here for Miss Kelso."

That letter simply had to be there! I said: "How about another delivery? Is it possible that the letter would be delivered later in the day?"

"Not unless it's special delivery."

By God, I thought, that would really cook me, if that letter turned out to be special delivery. But surely Ellen Foster would have noticed a thing like that—sure she would—so I immediately ruled out the possibility of special delivery.

The postman gave me one look, a sort of fishy look, then turned and went out of the building. It was all I could do to keep from yelling at him and making him go through his bag all over again. That letter just *had* to be there somewhere!

But it wasn't. If that letter had fallen into the wrong hands, I was good as dead, and I didn't want to admit it.

What I had to do was think. This was no time for breast beating and wailing. I stood there staring at the mail box, that empty mail box, and made myself calm down. There was one thing I had to do; I had to systematically figure out what had happened to that letter.

Now that letter was mailed around four o'clock yesterday afternoon ... that's the starting point. There was just a chance that the letter wasn't picked up at all yesterday. If that was the case, it wouldn't be delivered until tomorrow, since there was only one-a-day delivery service at this address. Maybe that's what happened, I thought. And I began to feel better.

But only for an instant. Oh, no, I thought, that letter was picked up all right. If it hadn't been, the police would have intercepted it right on the spot.

That left two possibilities, two possible explanations as to why the letter hadn't arrived here this morning: either it had been lost, or it had been intercepted at the main mail distribution point.

Then I thought: what are the odds on getting a letter lost in the mails? A million to one? Two million to one? The post office is a damned efficient organization; they just don't lose letters, especially on local delivery, often enough to make it a possibility.

That left only one answer, the answer that I had been trying to dodge, the answer that I was afraid of. *The letter had been intercepted by the police.* I didn't know how, but it had happened!

I had promised myself that I would never be afraid again ... but I was afraid now.

It was a miracle that I was still alive! The miracle was that this apartment building hadn't been swarming with cops long before now! By God, I thought, I've got to get out of here! I've got to move faster than I ever moved in my life!

That was when I started running.

I suppose I was running for my apartment, but I can't be sure about anything that happened for the next few minutes. Panic had seized me and for that instant had complete control of me, but instinct alone had probably turned me toward my apartment. That's where my money was. That's where my gun was—the equipment of survival.

Once I recognized the fact that the letter had been intercepted, I knew instantly just the way it must have happened. It had started with that maid, Ellen Foster, who had suddenly become so proud of her memory. After thinking it over, she must have realized that the name on the letter hadn't been Keaslo at all, but Kelso, and she had probably called the cops about it.

But it couldn't have happened last night. It could only have happened this morning, and not early this morning, either, and that was the only thing that saved me this long. That and a legal complication that naturally arises when you fool with the U. S. Mail. The cops, after they had intercepted the letter, probably had gone after Pat's permission to open it and act on the information in it. That small time lapse had saved me. It had given the postman time to make his regular delivery and arouse my suspicions.

If the cops had just held up that postman I would have been cooked hours ago. Blue suits and badges would have filled my apartment before I'd even got out of bed.

All this went through my mind as I ran down the hallway of that apartment building. In a matter of seconds the whole story was there, full grown, in front of me.

But the situation was bad enough as it was. Sooner or later the cops would be here. In a matter of minutes, probably, or even seconds. Surely, they would know the contents of Dorris Venci's letter by this time, the news that Roy Surratt, Alex Burton's murderer, was at large in Lake City. I didn't dare think of the number of police cars that must be converging on this point at this minute, this second.

Where I was going from the apartment I didn't know. I just knew instinctively that I had to get there first, I had to get the gun, the money, the keys to the Lincoln. I didn't have enough of a future to plan on ... the future, after I had picked up the essentials, would have to take care of itself.

I was about six or eight quick running steps from the mailbox, right at the rear entrance of the apartment building, when I heard the first siren.

The sound froze me.

I forgot about the apartment. I forgot, gun, money, keys, everything. All I could think about was getting away from there as fast as possible. I hit the rear entrance of the apartment building with a force that almost took the door off the hinges. I ran past the garage stall where the Lincoln was parked ... that sleek, beautiful, powerful Lincoln that I'd never be able to use again, not even if I had remembered the keys. They would be looking for that Lincoln, they would be looking for any kind of car, so I didn't even give it a second glance.

I ran around the row of brick garage stalls, clawed my way through a hedge fence and broke into the open alley behind the apartment building. I had no time to wonder where I was going from here. The first siren was getting louder now, much louder, and others were beginning to join the screeching chorus. I only knew that I had to keep running until I could no longer hear the sirens, and then maybe I could stop for a moment and think.

I darted across the alley and plowed through another hedge fence, and there on the other side of the fence was another string of second-rate apartment buildings, much like the one I had lived in. I ran blindly, headed nowhere in particular, just running in panic. It was like a nightmare, the harder I ran the closer the sirens got. I circled the apartment buildings and crossed the street which placed me a block away from where I had started. A woman coming out of a drugstore stopped to watch, but I ducked behind another building at the end of the block and didn't see her again.

I began to think about Dorris Venci as I ran. Goddamn that warped brain of hers!

But it was too late for regrets. Too late for anything but running, so I ran.

I stopped in a doorway and tried to get my breath, but the sound of those sirens wouldn't let me rest. Every god-damned car on the force must be answering this call! I thought. Well, who could blame them? It's not every day that you get a chance to pick up Roy Surratt, defenseless and alone, the way he is now!

But I kept telling myself: You've got to stop this running! It's idiotic, all this running when you don't even know where you're going! It only attracts attention.

When the prowl car went past, sirens screaming, four or five people came out of a supermarket to see what was going on. I joined them.

"Land sakes!" a woman was saying. "Where are the fire trucks?"

"It's not a fire," a young guy in a white apron said. "It's a police car, I just saw it go by."

"Well, I never heard the likes! What do you suppose ..."

I was afraid they would notice how out of breath I was. I eased to the edge of the group and into another doorway. *Now what are you going to do, Surratt? You're the genius. The perfectionist. The criminal philosopher. You're the one who talks so much about the use of brains and au-dacity. Well, let's see you get out of this one, if you're so goddamn smart!*

That little pep talk did me more good than anything that could possibly have happened; it stilled the panic; it gave me time to think.

All right, I thought savagely, I'll get out of this yet! How about that little business with Calvart? I'd never be in a spot tighter than that one if I lived to be a thousand!

I felt a little better. I didn't feel so much like a pile of quivering mush. What I needed right now was a friend. A good, strong friend like John Venci ... but Venci was dead. I didn't have a friend, I didn't even have an acquaintance that I could go to for help.

It was Roy Surratt against the world.

By now the people who had come out of the supermarket had gone back in, or had drifted away. I stood there in the doorway wondering what the hell I was going to do. I had to get out of this neighborhood somehow, and fast, but I had no idea how I was going to manage it until I saw the young punk, the kid in the white apron, come out of the supermarket loaded down with two paper bags full of groceries. There was a Ford sedan at the curb in front of the supermarket, and that's where he was heading.

"Just a minute, Joe, I'll get that door for you."

I looked around to see where the voice was coming from, and saw the woman coming out of the market carrying another, smaller, bag. She was about forty years old and looked like a typical middleclass housewife. She opened the luggage compartment and the kid dumped the groceries inside.

"Thanks, Mrs. Rider. That canned stuff sure is heavy." The woman said something and the kid went back to the supermarket. Mrs. Rider stood there for a minute, frowning and listening to the sirens, then she closed the trunk lid that the punk had forgotten and went around to the driver's side of the car. I stepped out of the doorway and walked over to the Ford.

"There's been no accident, Mrs. Rider," I said.

Startled, she snapped her head around and stared at me. "I beg your pardon?"

"I said there's been no accident. Those police cars you hear, they're looking for me, Mrs. Rider." I didn't have a gun to freeze her into silence, and I didn't want her to start screaming ... not until I was close enough to choke it off, at least. So I spoke gently, quietly, hoping that she would understand her position and be sensible about it.

I opened the door on the driver's side and said, "I don't want to hurt you, Mrs. Rider. That's the last thing in the world I want...." But it was no use. I could see the scream coming up in her throat.

I had to act fast. I jumped inside and hit her. I knocked the scream out of her before it ever became a sound. Her head snapped back and she fell against the door on the other side of the car. I grabbed her and stuffed her down to the floorboards.

She was out cold.

CHAPTER EIGHTEEN

In the glove compartment I found an eight inch crescent wrench and a state road map. The wrench I slipped into my right hand pocket, the map I spread out on my lap and studied for four or five minutes trying to decide on the best escape route out of Lake City.

There were several ways to get out of the city, but the best and quickest way was a superhighway leading south of the city. Just outside the city limits there was an elaborate traffic circle that would take you off in about any direction you wanted, and I decided this would be my best bet. My big problem was getting to that traffic circle before the cops set up a roadblock.

I stuffed the road map back into the glove compartment

and then pulled Mrs. Rider up onto the seat and slapped her a couple of times to bring her out of it. She wasn't really hurt, although she might have trouble chewing on the left side of her jaw for a few days. She was suffering from shock more than anything. The slapping took care of that.

"... Stop that!"

"That's more like it," I grinned. I had slipped over on the passenger's side of the car and put her under the wheel, and now I had my hand in my coat pocket, holding the crescent wrench like a gun.

"Mrs. Rider," I said quietly, "I don't want to be forced to use this gun. Now you're not going to make me use the gun, are you?"

That scared her plenty, and I knew I had her in the palm of my hand. "Please ... please put it away!"

"It's just a precaution, Mrs. Rider; a man in my position can't afford to take chances."

"What ... are you going to do!"

"I've got to get out of Lake City, and I've got to do it fast. You're going to help me, Mrs. Rider. You are going to drive just where I tell you to drive, and as long as you do that you won't be hurt."

"I'm ... I'm so nervous ... I don't think I can drive."

"Sure you can, Mrs. Rider. All you have to do is keep thinking about this gun in my pocket. You keep thinking about this gun, and what will happen to you if anything goes wrong, and I'm sure everything will be fine. Now start the car."

She was nervous, all right, but she started the car. She was thoroughly convinced that I had a gun on her, and would kill her, and she was more than eager to do anything I said.

I directed her west, through the outskirts of Lake City, and then we hit the four lane highway and headed south and I stopped worrying about Mrs. Rider. But I worried about those cops, plenty.

Those cops with their short wave radios, and their tele-type machines, and their identification experts. What I needed was a short wave radio, one like Dorris Venci had had in her Lincoln. If I had a radio like that, I'd know if the cops were already busy setting up roadblocks or if they were still fooling around that apartment house trying to flush me out of some hole.

But I didn't have a radio and I didn't know a damn thing. All I could do was hope.

Then I glanced at the Ford's speedometer and it was nosing up toward 60, and I said sharply, "Watch your speed!"

She winced as though I had slapped her again, but she jumped off that accelerator. "Please!" she said, almost sobbing. "You know how nervous I am!"

"And you know how cops are about speed laws. If we get jumped for speeding, Mrs. Rider, I'll be forced to con-clude that you did it on purpose and act accordingly. That's something you might think over whenever you see that speedometer indicate more than 45."

"I just didn't notice!" she whined. "I had no idea of att-racting the police!"

"I assure you," I told her, "that such an idea would be a most dangerous one."

Several minutes went by. We said nothing. There wasn't a cop in sight, anywhere. After a while I got to thinking, maybe it's going to work! Maybe I got the jump on them enough to make it work!

Then, at that moment when I should have been thinking "cops" and nothing but "cops," I found myself thinking about Pat.

That's all over now, I thought. Even before it got started, it's over. And I felt a kind of emptiness that I had never known before. By now she probably knew all about me. By now she would know that I had killed Alex Burton, and she was probably hating my guts like she had never hated anything before.

Strangely, that was my only regret at that moment. All around me were the cops, I was just a short jump ahead of violent death and I knew it ... what's more, I had just seen my beautiful million dollar blackmail scheme go down the sewer ... still, all I could think of was that Pat was hating my guts.

I didn't know if I loved her ... or even if I was capable of love; but all the same the emptiness was there, cold and swollen inside me. Then I caught myself toying with a dangerous idea, much more dangerous than the one I had warned Mrs. Rider about. I caught myself thinking: If I could just see her and talk to her maybe I could get it straightened out. After all, she has nothing to go on but Dorris's letter; so it's my word against Dorris's word. And Dorris Venci, I reminded myself, had never given her a Balmain coat, and I had. That should make a difference about whose word she would take, if I knew anything at all about women.

I had seen Pat's eyes, that night when she had stood staring at herself in my mirror, all wrapped up in the fantastic luxury of that coat. I remembered that night and seriously doubted that my past, my prison record, would bother her a great deal.

Then Mrs. Rider made a small surprised sound and the car began to slow down.

I snapped out of it. I slammed the door on my subconscious.

"What are you doing!"

"... Up ahead" she said shakily, licking her lips nervously. "The traffic ..."

I saw it then, and my heart hammered against my ribs about three times and then seemed to stop. About three or four hundred yards down the highway traffic was beginning to pile up ... and nobody had to tell me what that meant.

The police had got a jump ahead of me. They had already set up a roadblock!

I could feel my world going to pieces right under my feet. Jesus! I thought, what am I going to do now!

But this time I held panic off with both hands. This is only the beginning, I reminded myself. This is a bad spot, but there are going to be plenty of bad spots before you get out of this mess, so you might as well learn to take them.

I grabbed the steering wheel and pulled with everything I had.

Mrs. Rider screamed. I thought the Ford was coming apart as we hit the raised concrete island that divided the four lane highway, but we got across it somehow. I heard tires screech like ripping canvas as the stream of north-bound traffic tried to jam into the outside lane to keep from broadsiding us.

I didn't give a damn about the traffic. I yelled at Mrs. Rider: "Floorboard it!"

Now I was perfectly cool and she was the nervous wreck. But when I made a move toward my right pocket she made a tight, squealing little sound and jammed the accelerator to the floor.

"Goddamnit," I yelled, "take the steering wheel!"

Half scared to death, she took the wheel from me and the car heeled dangerously as she fought to get it under control. She finally got it straightened out without once taking her foot from the accelerator.

I looked back and saw that all the traffic far behind us was now crowding over to the outside lane. That meant that the cops had seen us trying to escape the roadblock. They had opened up with the sirens and were getting ready to come after us.

Well, let them come! Now that the action had started I was perfectly calm. I glimpsed the flashing red light on top of the police car, but we had a good jump on them. They weren't nearly close enough to start shooting, and I didn't intend for them to get that close.

"Faster!" I shouted.

"I ... I can't go any faster! The car won't go any faster!" Her voice was a high-pitched whine, almost like a siren. This, I thought, will be a day she'll never forget! This will be a day she can tell her grandchildren about—if she's smart and stays alive long enough to have any grandchildren.

I studied the road ahead for a moment, watching the city rushing toward us. I looked back at the cops and saw that they were closing some ground, but not enough to catch us for a while. At last I glanced at Mrs. Rider's white face.

"How well do you know this town?"

She worked her mouth but the words simply wouldn't come out.

I said, "I want you to take the next through street to the right, heading right for the heart of town. You understand me?"

She nodded, blinking her eyes rapidly. Goddamn you, I thought, you better not start crying! Not while you're driving this car! About five or six hundred yards up the highway she braked and bent the Ford hard to the right. She damn near rolled it—there was an eerie, floating sensation as both left wheels went up in the air.

However, this was Mrs. Rider's lucky day. This was her day to stay alive, in spite of everything. She took that corner like a champ at the Indianapolis races.

My heart was in my throat. "Goddamnit!" I started to yell, "this is no race you're driving!" Then I changed my mind and said nothing. This was her lucky day, let her ride it out.

I looked back and couldn't see the police car—but this was no permanent arrangement and I knew it. We were now in a part of Lake City that I had never seen before, a warehouse district with several big tractor and trailer jobs parked along the shoulders. I said, "Turn left, that next street up ahead." I wanted to get off this through street before the cops made their turn from the highway. There was no use wondering where we went from there. The best plan in the world was no good now—I'd just have to make it up as I went along.

Still, I knew something had to be done, and fast. You simply don't barrel through a place like Lake City at 60 miles an hour, with a cop car on your tail, without attracting some attention. The way things were now going, it was only a matter of time before the end came, and not much time at that.

Well ... there was no time like the present.

"This will do," I said.

She didn't understand me, or maybe she was concentrating so hard on her driving that she didn't hear.

"Stop the car!" I said. And this time she understood. She shot a panic stricken glance at me and began breaking to a stop.

"Now get out," I said, reaching in front of her and opening the door. The car had barely come to a stop when I gave her a shove and that was the last I saw of Mrs. Rider. The longer I kept her with me the higher the odds became that sooner or later she would do something crazy and I would have to kill her. I wondered if Mrs. Rider appreciated the favor I'd done her. Probably she was worrying more about the groceries in the luggage compartment—that's the way women's minds seem to work.

I forgot about Mrs. Rider completely. I'd lost the cops for a few minutes, but only for a very few minutes. Already they would have radioed for help and in a very short time this part of Lake City was going to be swarming with police.

Strangely enough, I was perfectly cool now, my mind

operating with the clean precision of an electronic calculator. This car, like its owner, had now become more of a liability than an asset—the big problem right now was getting it off my hands. But the cops would find it sure if I just parked it and got out; then they would know that I had to be in the immediate neighborhood.

By now I was about four blocks from where I'd dumped Mrs. Rider, and ahead of me there was a sign:

RED BALL GARAGE
DAY AND NIGHT WRECKER SERVICE
WE FIX FLATS.

I turned the Ford into the big open doorway of the garage. When the motor died I could hear the sirens—more than one now. Then I noticed a black bag on the floorboards and picked it up. Inside there was a five dollar bill and some change—not much, but certainly better than nothing. Mrs. Rider, I thought with an almost hysterical gayety, don't think I don't appreciate this! I pocketed the money and felt an insane impulse to giggle.

I got out of the Ford and walked over to where a big man in grease-stained coveralls had his head under the hood of a new De Soto.

CHAPTER NINETEEN

I said, "How long will it take to get a valve and ring job on this Ford?"

The mechanic took his head out of the De Soto. "Maybe tomorrow I can get started. Maybe this afternoon."

"No hurry, no hurry at all," I said pleasantly. "What I want is a good job. I don't care how long it takes."

He shrugged. "All right, tomorrow." Then he screwed up his face, thoughtfully, listening. "Sounds like a fire out there," he said, finally getting around to hearing the sirens.

I preferred to ignore the sirens for the present. "It will be all right to leave the Ford here in the garage, won't it?"

"Sure.... Sure," he said vaguely, still listening.

There were three or four of them now, and from what I could hear, they were moving toward the north, away from the warehouse district, still looking for that Ford.

Well, that suited me fine. I figured it would take a while before they got around to checking the garages, and by that time I hoped to be far away from this part of town; far away from Lake City. I got the mechanic to make out a ticket on the repairs he thought I wanted on the Ford, valve job, new rings, the works, and then I signed a phony name and got out of there. Yes sir, I thought, it's going to take them a while to trace that Ford.

I walked out to the sidewalk and stood there listening, and the sound of the sirens was just a whisper now, just a hint of a scream in the distance. I felt secure for the moment, but I knew that wasn't going to last. The odds against me were growing fast. The impulse to run, run blindly, was almost irresistible, but I put it down. If I had taken time to think at the beginning I would be in a much better position at this moment: I'd have a gun; I'd have a bankroll; I'd be in a position to help myself.

Well, there was no use crying about it now. I had to figure out a way to get out of here, far away, and I could allow nothing else to occupy my mind until that was settled.

I moved down the sidewalk, cautiously, but not too cautiously, not so cautiously as to attract attention. I kept my eyes open; I regarded everything that crossed my line of vision as a possible instrument of escape. Just stay calm, I kept telling myself, and something will show up, something always shows up to those who wait. Then I saw something and thought, this is it!

What I saw was a railroad track—not the main tracks but a spur line that served the warehouse district—and when I reached the end of the block, I saw the lineup of freight cars and flatcars pulled off on the siding, and a small fleet of big tractor-semi jobs loading, unloading, coming, going. It looked like a busy place, and up ahead there was an old fashioned coal burning switch engine, and that started me thinking.

A switch engine.... It must mean that the line of freight cars was being readied to leave Lake City. That's just what's going to happen, I thought. Those cars are going to be coupled together, that switch engine would move the whole string out to the main track where it would become a part of the outgoing freight train getting ready to pull out right at this moment.

And that was when I saw the cops. A big job pulled away from the track, and there on the other side of the truck was a black and white sedan, a red warning light on top, a long, waving short wave antenna at the rear. A squad car, all right. I was old enough to know a squad car when I saw one!

Well, I thought, almost tempted to smile, they are a very efficient crew, these Lake City Police. First roadblocks, now they are searching freight cars, and no doubt they already had men working the bus stations, depots, and even the airfields.

Let them search. Let them get it out of their systems—I was just glad they had decided to do it now instead of a few minutes later, because in a few minutes I intended to be in one of those freight cars. I intended to punch myself a one way ticket to Los Angeles, Philadelphia, Detroit, anywhere. I didn't care where it was, just so the name wasn't Lake City.

What I needed was breathing space, thinking time—and those cops were fixing it up very nicely. It didn't occur to me that their searching the train at this particular time was a very close call; what occurred to me was that my luck must be changing. It *must* be changing! Surely they wouldn't come back and search that train again, after having done it once....

Yes sir, the cards were beginning to fall!

I waited patiently, watching the activity at the tracks, and after a while I saw the cops, two of them, climb out of a box car and drive away.

As soon as the police car was out of sight I began walking toward the track. Not a detail did I miss, for details were what my future hinged on. Details could mean the difference between living and dying. So I noted carefully that there were eighteen cars, four of them flatcars, two refrigerated cars, and the others were ordinary red-painted box cars.

Those box cars are out, I thought immediately. They load those things and lock them tight before they are coupled with the train ... and I sure didn't want to find myself a prisoner in a box car. The refrigerated cars were out too. They offered the advantage of having ventilating and icing doors at the top, but too many people were apt to get curious about the contents of a refrigerated car, so that left only the flatcars, which didn't seem very promising at first.

But that changed when I saw the two workmen stretching the big gray tarp over the tractors. They were bright red high-wheeled farm tractors, four of them anchored down with cables and pulleys on one of the flatcars, and now the workmen were stretching the big tarp over them so they would look nice and new when they got to wherever they were going.

It didn't take the workmen long to get the tarp lashed down to everyone's satisfaction. They dropped off the flatcar, got in a truck and drove away. Most of the trucks and workmen were gone now ... it looked like the cars were loaded and ready to pull out.

Sure enough, the switch engine began backing up, the engineer leaning out the far side of the cab to get his signals from the brakeman.

Now! I thought. It's now or never if you want to get out of Lake City alive! I broke into a jog, being careful to keep a box car between me and the brakeman. I swung up to the flatcar and squeezed under the edge of the tarp.

This was the dangerous time. This was a time for holding my breath and hoping that brakeman hadn't seen me. Apparently he hadn't. Nobody yelled, nobody stuck his head under the tarp to see what the hell I was doing there, so apparently I had brought it off perfectly and nobody at all had seen me.

I breathed easier ... everything was coming out just right. Of course this flatcar couldn't be called first class travel, but it would do. Up ahead I could hear the cars coming together, coupling, with teeth-jarring rattles. And then the car directly ahead smashed into my flatcar and slammed me back against one of the tractors. One of the big lugs on the tractor's rear wheel tore my coat as I grabbed for something to hold to—but that didn't bother me. Nothing could bother me now. I was as good as out of Lake City! In spite of the police, in spite of their elaborate communication system and their roadblocks!

At last the entire string of cars was coupled together and we began to move forward. We moved forward for maybe ten minutes, then stopped. Then we moved in reverse for a short distance, then forward again. I couldn't see what was going on, but I knew that a certain amount of switching had to be done to get us on the right track.

I don't know how many times we went forward, stopped, then went backward and finally forward again. It seemed like a long time, as I crouched there under the tarp in semi-darkness, being slammed against the steel of those tractors every time the engineer changed directions. Finally we stopped and this time we didn't move again. I heard the switch engine break off and move away by itself.

It won't be long now, I thought. We're on the right track, now all I have to do is wait.

I waited for what seemed like hours and nothing happened. Nothing at all. Every so often I could hear somebody crunch past on the cinders beside the track, and I died a little every time, and thought: What the hell am I going to do if it's a railroad inspector and he sticks his head under this tarp, or the cops coming back for a second look! But they always went on, and after a while my heart would start beating normally again.

If only I had a gun, I kept thinking...

But I didn't have a gun.

And what was holding up this string of cars? Why didn't a train pick it up and get it moving?

I didn't know the answer, and I didn't dare stick my head under that tarp to try to find out. I crouched there, and the long minutes and hours crawled by, and at last I realized that the sun had moved from one side to the other on the tarp and that at least four or five hours must have gone by since I first swung onto this flatcar that I was now beginning to hate.

That was when I finally realized that that string of cars wasn't going anywhere. Not today, anyway. Maybe not for a week, or even a month!

The realization came slowly, but probably it had been in the back of my mind all along and I had simply refused to look at it. But there was no getting around it now. I was stuck! I was on a train going nowhere!

At that moment I was utterly defeated. All I could think of was—this is the end of the line! The hand had been played out.

For several minutes, maybe longer, I wallowed in the muck and slime of self-pity—but finally I pulled myself out of that. By God, I told myself, I've *got* to get myself out of this!

But one thought kept hammering at me. Jesus, if I only

had a gun! I was rapidly becoming a nut on the idea of not having a gun. What I needed right now was a friend like John Venci to give me a gun and a bankroll.

I might as well have wished for a platinum plated key to Fort Knox. No sir, I thought, it's going to take more than wishing to get out of this, Surratt....

Then one word, one name crossed my mind.... *Pat!*

I hadn't dared think of her until now. The minute that letter had been intercepted I made myself stop thinking about her. No matter what I had felt about her, or what she had felt about me, I had to accept the fact that Pat must now hate my guts because she knew that I had killed Alex Burton.

But now I started thinking in a new direction, almost another dimension.

The question I asked myself was: Did Pat actually *know* that I had killed Burton? All she had was the word of an unbalanced woman, to put it kindly, and was there any particular reason that she should take the word of a gangster's wife against mine?

Jesus, I thought, the excitement of the idea beginning to grip me, I wonder if I actually could bring her around! I wonder if I could somehow make her believe that I had nothing to do with that Burton killing!

The fact was, I had very little choice in the matter. My position right now was much the same as it had been in prison. Lake City was my prison, all exits were locked to me, and to crash out successfully I simply had to have help ... and Pat was the only possible person who might give it.

I could hear my every heartbeat as I crouched there by the tractors. If I bring this off, I thought, it will be the most audacious action of my career.

However, any debate on the matter would be purely academic, for Pat held my life in her hands. Either she would help me, or she wouldn't. Either I would die, or I wouldn't.

Strangely enough I was perfectly calm as I considered the possibilities. *The first thing I've got to do is get to a phone,* I thought. *I've got to contact Pat and I've got to give the most convincing performance of my life!*

Beyond that point there was no sense making plans.

In the distance I could hear those out-of-tune electronic chimes banging out every quarter hour. The distance that those discordant sounds could cover was positively amazing, but at least they were functional. By paying attention to the chimes I now knew that it was five o'clock and that seven full hours had passed since the police cars had first started closing in on my apartment.

Only seven hours? It seemed like a lifetime ago!

Getting started was the tough part. I had begun to associate a feeling of security with this flatcar. I began to hate the thought of leaving it. I began to think what a nice thing it would be if I could curl up into a tight little knot and lie there in the quiet darkness and pretend that everything was going to work out fine, just the way it was, and it really wasn't necessary to return to that jungle fury that lay on the other side of the tarp.

I lifted the tarp just a little and looked outside. Just as I had figured, the string of cars had been left on a siding. I looked out at an amazing network of steel tracks only slightly less complicated than the human nerve system, and beyond the tracks there were several sprawling red-brick buildings and a high wire fence. I had a look on the other side of the car and decided this would be my best bet. In this direction there were very few tracks. There was a maze of cattle pens and loading chutes. Most of the cattle pens were empty and there was no sign of unusual activity—certainly there were no cops in sight.

Well, I thought, I might as well take the plunge.

CHAPTER TWENTY

The afternoon papers were in a wire rack in front of a drugstore and I could read the headlines from half a block away. KILLER LOOSE IN LAKE CITY.

I'd been almost an hour getting completely away from the freight yards, finding my way out of that maze of cattle pens and trying to watch out for cops at the same time. I had finally made it this far, maybe two or three blocks away from the yards, to that crummy, down-at-the-heel section of the city that always seems to thrive close to the tracks. I had made it this far with no trouble. Not a single pair of eyes had given me a second glance, and just as I was feeling that everything was going nicely, that headline hit me. What really jarred me was the picture. I had never been news like this before—I wasn't accustomed to seeing a three column cut of myself on the front page just below a black two inch screamer.

Are all these people blind! I thought. How can they look at me and fail to recognize me as the "killer"?

Then I looked at myself in a plateglass window and understood. The man I saw in the glass was not the best looking man in the world, and certainly not the neatest, but he was wearing a good suit, a tie, a shirt with a button-down collar. Even I had trouble believing that the man who had sat for those prison mug shots in the paper could be the same man looking back at me from the plateglass window. Well, I'll be damned! I felt an impulse to laugh.

But I put it down immediately.

A trained eye, a cop's eye, would spot me in an instant ... and the cops were the only ones who counted in this game of life and death that I was playing. Don't forget that, Surratt. Don't forget it for an instant!

I didn't forget it, but I did feel a little better until a cop stepped onto the sidewalk about four doors down from where I was standing!

My heart stopped still. He was a big sonofabitch, two hundred at least; he had just stepped out of a chili joint and still had a toothpick in his mouth. He wiped his mouth, then planted himself solidly in the middle of the sidewalk and glared hard at some point in the distance that seemed to anger him.

You stay just like that, I thought, easing into a doorway. You turn your head, you fix those steel-ball eyes of yours on my face, copper, and you'll be the deadest sonofabitch in Lake City!

It was complete nonsense, of course, because I had no gun and I certainly couldn't have handled a cop his size with my bare hands ... but it made me feel a little better just thinking it. As I thought it I eased into the doorway. I reached behind me and opened a door. Make it look natural, I told myself, as I turned and stepped through the doorway into what seemed to be another hash house.

The last I saw of that cop he was still standing there in that same spot, rocking slightly on the balls of his feet, his gaze still fixed angrily on that uncertain point in the distance. Maybe his feet hurt. Maybe he was mad because the captain had passed him over for promotion. You just keep thinking about it, I thought, whatever it is.

I closed the door and began to breathe again.

There was a woman behind the counter who looked at me when I came in but all she saw was just another drifter, in a world of drifters, who might be worth the price of coffee and sinkers, but that was all. There were two customers at the counter having the house special, stew, but they were too busy eating to be curious.

I headed for the phone booth.

I was perfectly calm until I dropped the coin in the slot and began to dial. That was when my insides began to crawl, that was when I fully realized how important these next few minutes or seconds could be to me. They could mean that I would either live or die—that's how important they were! All Pat had to say was "no" and I was dead. Just as sure as she could point a pistol at my head and pull the trigger. She could kill me. I absolutely had to have her help or I was cooked, really cooked this time, and nobody was more aware of that fact than I.

Of course that wasn't all I had to worry about. I had the cops to think of—all those cops with their elaborate organization. How much did they really know or could guess about me and Pat? Were they guessing enough to figure it would be a paying proposition to tap her telephone? If they were, I was still cooked. I might as well go back to the flatcar and wait for the end.

Those were a few of the things that went through my mind at that moment, but I kept dialing. There was nothing else to do.

I listened to the ringing at the other end. Once ... twice ... three times ... I listened so hard that I began to imagine that I could hear someone breathing on the line. But that was not possible. If Pat was playing seriously with the cops, and they had her line tapped, I would know it. They would have an extension connected and would try to lift the receivers at the same exact instant, and a man on the other end could tell when two circuits were opened instead of one, if he only listened hard enough.

I kept telling myself that I could tell the difference, but every time that phone rang at the other end I became less and less sure of myself. Four times it rang ... Five times....

Why didn't she answer? If she was in the apartment, certainly she would have had plenty of time to get to the phone by now! It hadn't occurred to me that she might not be in the apartment. It simply hadn't occurred to me that she wouldn't be there when I needed her!

Six times the phone rang.... Still no answer.

I wanted to hang up and get out of there. Every instinct

told me that something was wrong—maybe the cops were holding things up for some reason. Maybe they were putting their tracer to work, or maybe they simply had got their equipment fouled somehow, but with every second that passed I felt it stronger and stronger. Something was wrong.

Then the receiver came off the hook. It was absolutely clean. *Click*, and it was off, and Pat's voice was saying:

"... Hello?"

It was a strange thing, the way I felt at that moment. I forgot the cops, I forgot all fear for that instant, as Pat's voice sounded in the receiver—a quiet voice, somehow soothing the ragged edges of my nerves. For the first time, I guess, I was beginning to realize how much I missed her, how much I needed her. Not just for the present, as a means of escape, but really needed her.

"Pat," I said quickly, "don't hang up! Please don't hang up until I've explained something! It's very important!"

I didn't know how much the cops had worked on her; I didn't know how many of the papers she had read or how much she had believed. I was taking no chances. I simply couldn't let her hang up until I had a chance to convince her that I hadn't killed Alex Burton.

"Pat, do you hear me!"

For one long moment she said nothing. I was afraid that she was going to hang up. I was afraid that she wasn't going to give me a chance to talk her around ... and there was nothing I could do to stop it. All she had to do was replace the receiver, refuse to talk to me....

At last she said, "The police were just here, they left just a few moments ago." There was nothing soothing in her voice now. It was tightly drawn and rough with hate. "They'll find you, and I hope it's soon. It can't be too soon to suit me!"

"Listen to me!" I said, the words coming as fast as I could talk. "Pat, you've simply got to listen to me! I know what the cops have been telling you, and I know what you've been reading in the papers, but those things simply aren't true, not all of them anyway. You'll listen to me, won't you, for old times' sake if for nothing else?"

She made no sound at all.

"Sure," I rushed on, "my name is Roy Surratt, and once I killed a lousy sadist, a guard named Gorgan, but even that was in self-defense. I don't care what the cops told you or what you read in the newspapers. I didn't have anything to do with that Burton killing!"

This time she did make a small sound, a very small sound that meant absolutely nothing except possibly a kind of bitter interest had been aroused.

But I wasn't getting anywhere. I could feel it. Maybe I was crazy about her, but that didn't mean that she had to feel the same toward me. Oh, no, I was thinking, this is no time to kid yourself about a thing like that, Surratt. The only real tie you ever had to her was money, money that could buy Lincolns and Paris coats. So don't get the idea that soft soap will bring her around. Money, that's the thing women understand!

"Now listen to me, please!" I said. "This is very important; my life depends on it. Maybe your future depends on it, too, Pat. I'm going to tell you the truth, the absolute truth, so will you listen?"

She didn't say yes, but she didn't say no, either. I had the feeling that she was holding her breath ... waiting.

"All right," I went on quickly, "do you remember what I said about giving this town a shaking? Well, that's just what I did. I had it by the throat, I had the sweetest, most lucrative setup a man can imagine, but ... Well, something went wrong. What I'm trying to say is this: I need help, but I'm ready to pay for it. I'm not asking you to take chances for the sake of friendship or anything like that. I'm ready to pay."

But I was getting the uneasy feeling that she wasn't even

listening. Goddamnit, I thought savagely, what have I got to do to make her listen to me! I could almost see her, standing there like a stone-cold statue, as unfeeling and deaf as a statue. "Jesus!" I said, "won't you please listen to me, Pat! Are you still thinking about Burton; is that what's bothering you?"

Still she said nothing.

"Look," I said quickly, changing directions again, "you're not going to believe anything Dorris Venci said, are you? Let me tell you something about Dorris Venci; she was nuts! Absolutely and completely nuts! Somehow she got the crazy idea that she loved me, and that's the reason she wrote you the letter. I brushed her off and that burned her up. She wanted to hurt me, so she wrote you that letter full of lies."

I tried to think of something to add, but I had said just about everything there was to say. I could feel the ground falling out from under me. I understood perfectly well that my story was full of holes, but I could have plugged the holes if only she had given me a chance.

I felt completely helpless. And then, at last, she spoke. Her voice sounded as though it were coming all the way from the moon.

"... What kind of help ... do you want?"

I almost collapsed with relief. My heart began to pump again. "A gun," I said, before she could change her mind. "A revolver if you can find one, but this is not my day to be particular, just so it's a gun. And some cartridges to fit the gun. And a good road map of the state—a really good one, the kind they sell in drugstores for a dollar or so—and a car. I don't care what kind of a car, just so it runs and isn't hot."

"... Is that all?"

Christ! I thought, what a woman she is! I ask for the sun and the moon and the stars, and she wants to know is that all! "Yes," I said, "that's quite all. With a car and a gun and a good map to tell me where they're likely to throw up their roadblocks, a division of Marines couldn't stop me!"

"... The map will be simple," she said flatly. "I have a small automatic myself—.25 caliber, I believe it is—and some cartridges...."

I wasn't exactly an amateur with a gun; you don't have to have a cannon to stop a man, if you know how to shoot. "The automatic will do fine. What about the car?"

"I know a used car lot that will still be open. I've been shopping there for an inexpensive car for my own use— there shouldn't be any trouble."

Yes, I thought, with surprising bitterness, I suppose you will need a car of your own now. "The used car lot sounds right," I said. "How long do you think it will take?"

"... An hour, perhaps. More important is the expense— it will take a good deal of money, most of my savings...."

I grinned and thought: By God, you were right all along, Surratt! Money's the thing that brings them around! I tried to think of a figure that would sound impressive but not ridiculous. "Don't you worry about the expense," I said. "I told you I was ready to pay. Ten thousand dollars, that's what it will be worth to you."

"... Where shall I meet you?"

"Harrison at Fourth Street, down by the tracks."

"In about an hour?"

"An hour will be perfect."

Only then did she hang up.

How do you like that! I thought. You'll never completely understand women, Surratt. You might as well admit it. One minute they're cold as stone, the next minute they're laying their necks on the block for you!

But Pat Kelso was quite a woman just the same. She was my kind of woman; she had just proved it. She was beautiful, she had class; and she didn't let a few personal scruples stand in her way when she saw a chance to pick up ten grand. But she was going to go right through the ceiling when she found out there was no ten grand!

Well, no matter how fast you try you can take just one step at a time, so I'd worry about that problem when I got to it. Very gently, I hung the receiver back on the hook, smiling.

At the counter I paid the waitress for the sandwich and coffee, had her put the sandwich in a bag and took it with me.

It was beginning to get dark outside—I was glad of that. Not that it made much difference. These people had lost the knack of seeing beyond their own noses, and not one out of ten thousand would have recognized me anyway. Cops—they were the only people to worry about.

So I was careful as I came out of the hash house and was glad to see that my blue suited friend down the block had plodded on his way. I noticed a springiness to my step that hadn't been there before. It was almost as though a heavy weight had been removed from my shoulders, and the world was once more a tolerable place to live in.

I ate my sandwich in a fifteen cent movie house on Harrison Street. I kept my eyes on a neon lighted clock to one side of the screen and thought: Now Pat has the gun in her bag; now she has the cartridges; now she is putting on her coat—not the Balmain coat, just a plain one—to go to the drugstore; now she's at the drugstore buying the map; now she's on her way to the car lot....

It was almost as though I could actually see her. Forty-five minutes to go. Thirty minutes to go. Christ, don't get into an argument with that car dealer! I thought. This is no time to haggle over prices. Pay the sonofabitch what he wants, but get the car!

Fifteen minutes to go.

I made myself sit there a few minutes longer. I was completely safe as long as I sat here in the darkness, but once I stepped out there on the street there was no way of knowing what would happen. No sense begging for trouble. Sit here and wait it out, that's the thing.

Ten minutes to go.

Surely, I thought, she has the car by now. The car dealer knows her and there should be a minimum of red tape. An hour she had said. Well, I had waited fifty minutes and couldn't take it any longer—I got up and walked out.

Outside the movie house there were the usual drifters, down-at-the-heel refugees from limbo, but no cops. Where are the cops, anyway? I thought. With a killer on the loose you'd think they'd have two cops on every corner. There wasn't a cop anywhere, as far as I could see. Maybe this was the night of the Policemen's Ball, or maybe they were too busy ogling prostitutes and shaking down bookies to bother with a mere killer. No matter what the reason, there were no cops in sight and that was the important thing. I stepped out onto the sidewalk and walked casually toward Fourth Street.

Fourth was a dark street, an ugly ditch that someone had plowed through a cement city and had forgotten to fill up. It wasn't much to look at but it suited me fine. I turned the corner at Harrison and strolled about a quarter of the way down Fourth. The sun had died. While I had been in the movie house darkness had come down on the city.

Darkness was a good thing. It was just what I'd ordered. I stood in the doorway of a darkened pawn shop and waited for Pat to come with a new option on my contract with destiny.

CHAPTER TWENTY-ONE

She hit the hour-mark right on the nose, as well as I could tell waiting there in the darkness. I saw a tan Ford pull up at the corner of Harrison and Fourth and I knew it was Pat; I could feel it. I could feel the elation bubbling up inside me. It's all over but the yelling, I thought. Soon I'll be out of this town for good!

I stepped out of the darkened doorway and waved and she saw me immediately. I felt like a million dollars. I could feel myself grinning. By God, I thought, not one man in ten thousand could bring off an escape like this—but I will! I can feel it in my bones!

It wasn't a new Ford, far from it, but it seemed to be running all right and that was the thing that mattered. I didn't have it in mind to outrun the police—I was going to outsmart them! Pat turned onto Fourth and I was waiting at the curb. I was inside before she had braked to a complete stop.

"I certainly am glad to see you!" I said. "For the first time in my life I was close to admitting defeat."

She glanced at me but said nothing, which didn't surprise me. She seemed nervous, but who wouldn't be nervous, considering the spot she had put herself on? But she was still the most beautiful woman I had ever seen, and I had a crazy impulse to grab her right there, and to hell with everything else.

That was one impulse that I squashed in a hurry. Another day, I thought. Another day when I've gone into business somewhere else; and then I'll really buy her that fleet of Lincolns; then we'll really begin to live, the two of us.

She put the Ford in gear and said, "Where do you want to go?"

"Someplace where you can get a taxi without too much trouble. You've done your share, and a fine job it was too. The rest is up to me."

"I know a place near Lincoln Avenue ... will that be all right?"

"Lincoln Avenue is fine. How about the gun; you brought it, didn't you?"

"It's in my pocket. I'll give it to you in a minute." Maybe

I should have noticed that everything was not as it should have been. Maybe I should have noticed the flatness of her voice, the coldness of her beautiful face ... but the fact is that I didn't notice; I was too busy congratulating myself. I was too busy devouring the beauty of her face to notice the coldness. And when I finally did notice, it was too late.

I was hardly aware that she had braked the Ford and was pulling up to the curb. Then she looked at me and there was something in her eyes that made me look around.

"Say, I thought Lincoln Avenue was more to the west."

"... It is," she said.

Then I saw the gun. But it was much, much too late to do me any good. It was a small gun; it looked almost like a toy, even in her small hand.

It was no toy. A .25 caliber slug can be an awfully big piece of lead if you catch it in the right place. I stared at the gun, and the muzzle was looking me right in the belly, pointed right at the soft midsection just below the center of the rib cage, just about where my liver would be.

"What is this?" I said. Trying not to sweat so much, trying not to see what was perfectly obvious. "If this isn't Lincoln Avenue, why did you stop?"

"Don't you know?"

"No, I don't know. And for Christ's sake, don't you know better than to point a gun at a person unless you mean to kill him?"

She almost smiled, but not quite.

Strangely, I was not scared. Certainly I was not so stupid that I did not recognize the situation for what it was. I had not convinced her of anything—that much was clear to me now. I had succeeded only in convincing myself that everything was going to be all right, because that was what I wanted to believe.

But not Pat. I hadn't fooled her for a minute. She was

just as sure as she had ever been that I had killed Alex Burton. When would I ever learn that it didn't pay to underrate women!

Maybe I would never get a chance to learn—for Pat meant to kill me. There was no doubt about it. She didn't mean for the electric chair to do it; she was going to do it herself.

Strangely, I was not afraid. I simply did not believe that a girl like Pat had the kind of guts it took to pull the trigger on another human being.

I made myself smile. I made myself think that it was some kind of fantastic joke. I made myself say quite calmly, "All right, you've got something on your mind. You might as well tell me about it now."

For one tense moment I thought she actually was going to shoot. I shifted my glance quickly from the gun to her face and was shocked to see that she was no longer beautiful. The hand of hate had strained and drawn her face almost beyond recognition—oh, there was plenty of hate there, more than enough to kill. But somehow I had the feeling that she was not going to pull the trigger.

I said, "Why don't you give me that automatic? You look pretty silly, and you know you're not going to use it."

"... You killed him." A voice without tone. A defeated voice, I thought. "The kindest, gentlest man I ever knew. The only man I ever loved. You killed him."

"But I explained all that," I said patiently. "When I talked to you. This crazy woman, this Dorris Venci, she wrote you that letter because she was mad at me. She knew how it was with you and Burton, a lot of people did. She knew that she could make you hate me if she could convince you that I had something to do with the Burton murder. That's exactly the reason she wrote the letter. You're much too sensible a girl to swallow a story like that."

"Mrs. Venci didn't even mention Alex Burton in her letter," Pat said flatly.

That stunned me.

"What did you say!"

"Mrs. Venci made no mention of Alex Burton. She identified you as Roy Surratt, an escaped convict, and warned me to have nothing to do with you."

"That was *all* she put in that letter!"

"That was all."

Jesus! I thought, what an idiot I've been! "Look … You've got this figured all wrong. I can explain it; believe me, I can!"

"Can you, Mr. Surratt?"

No, I couldn't. There was no way in the world to explain my way around a blunder as momentous as this one.

"Roy Surratt!" she said, staring right through me. "You actually believe, don't you, that you are some kind of superior being on this earth. You don't consider it necessary to answer to all us underlings for your actions, no matter what they may be. Roy Surratt! Master criminal! Philosopher!"

She laughed then, and it was not a pretty sound. "The gall of you! The *audacity!* How dare you behave as though you were the only person on earth possessed of the ability to think, to analyze, to define! Your enormous ego is your greatest weakness; did you know that? How could you have believed that you could kill a man like Alex Burton and get away with it?"

"Take it easy," I said soothingly, watching that automatic. "Just take it easy, won't you, and please remember that in this country a person is innocent until proven guilty."

"I know you are guilty," she said tightly. "I think I've known it from the first moment I saw you."

"That doesn't make much sense, does it? After all, you did go out with me. You did accept that coat, and you did enjoy my company. Does that sound as though you suspected me of killing your friend?"

Suddenly she smiled, and it was like no smile I had ever seen before. "That incredible ego! You believe what you want to believe and nothing else. Couldn't you see that the very sight of you made me sick!"

Just keep her talking, I thought. Sooner or later she will relax and I'll grab that gun. Then we'll see whether my ego's a weakness! I said, "How about the night I gave you the coat? Are you telling me that was an act too?"

I'd hit her with something that time. The color drained from her face and for an instant I thought she was going to collapse. But she didn't, and the automatic didn't waver. "... Yes," she said quietly, almost whispered, "... I wanted that coat. It represented something to me, it brought back memories of elegance, a way of life that I had once known."

I kept pushing. "And you still maintain that you suspected me all along of killing Burton?"

"... I'm thinking of the first time we met outside the apartment," she breathed, almost to herself. "In front of the factory office building, you were waiting there."

"I remember."

"You mentioned the night that Alex was killed. You noted the fact that Alex and I had been to the University Club and later the Crestview."

"Is there something wrong with that?"

"It was the first time I had been with Alex to either of those places. We ... weren't together much in public."

"I'll bet," I said, still with a bit of bitterness, remembering a certain chafing dish, a certain bedroom and photograph that I had hated, even before I had known that it was of Alex Burton.

"How did you know," she asked, "that Alex had taken me to those particular places on that particular night?"

"I don't know. Maybe I read it in the paper."

"It wasn't in the paper. No one knew, just a few club members and the police—not the kind of people you would associate with. You followed us that night, that's how you knew. You followed us, and after Alex left me at my apartment you killed him."

She didn't have to draw it any plainer than that. She had me pegged. She'd had me pegged from the very first. She had stuck to me, played up to me, waiting for me to make a mistake!

Well, I'd made the mistake.

It was strange—but I didn't seem to care. I didn't feel smart any more. I didn't feel like a Master Criminal. I didn't feel like a wise guy, either, who knew all the answers. All I felt was the emptiness. "... All right," I said finally, "I killed him. Is that what you want to hear? He was a lousy, thieving, no-good bastard, and I killed him."

That was when she shot me.

It was strange, but I didn't hear the explosion. That little automatic was no more than a foot away and I didn't even hear it. It was the shock, I suppose. The bullet went through me like a beam of light opening a path in the darkness. A very small piece of lead, not as large as your little finger. The impact knocked the breath out of me. I couldn't move my head. The entire lower part of my body was numb. My spinal column must be shattered, I thought. I wonder what's keeping me alive?

That was the last I remembered for a long, long while. Darkness closed in, and when I opened my eyes again it was in the white glare of a hospital room with cops standing around like angry statues, glaring down at me.

"What do you think?" someone asked.

And another voice said, "We can patch him up well enough to walk to the chair."

And that was when I stopped worrying about myself; my end was certain. I was aboard a slow freight bound for oblivion, my body half dead, only my brain fully alive. It's really too bad, I kept thinking. It's really quite a shame that it has to end this way because we'd have made a hell of a pair, Pat and I.

I didn't hate her. I no longer had the strength to support an emotion as violent as hate. The only thing left was a feeling of emptiness, a vague sort of incompleteness, a whispered fear that I had missed something somewhere along the line....

But it didn't matter now.

THE END

Clifton Adams was born in Comanche, Oklahoma in 1919. During WWII, he served in the Tank Corps in both Africa and Europe, developing his favorite hobby, cooking, while trying to prepare army rations. He wrote over 50 books and 125 stories under several pseudonyms—including Clay Randall, Jonathan Gant and Matt Kinkaid—

and won two Spur Awards for his westerns, *Tragg's Choice* in 1969 and *The Last Days of Wolf Garnett* in 1970. He had also been named "Oklahoma Writer of the Year" in 1965 by the University of Oklahoma, his alma mater. He died of a heart attack in San Francisco, California on October 7, 1971.

Clifton Adams Bibliography
(1919-1971)

Crime:
Whom Gods Destroy
  (1953)
Death's Sweet Song (1955)

As by Jonathan Gant
Never Say No to a Killer
  (1956)
The Long Vendetta (1963)

As by Nick Hudson
The Very Wicked (1960)

Westerns:
The Desperado (1950)
A Noose for the
  Desperado (1951)
The Colonel's Lady (1952)
Two-Gun Law (1954)
Gambling Man (1955)
Law of the Trigger (1956)
Outlaw's Son (1957)
Killer in Town (1959)
Stranger in Town (1960)

The Legend of Lonnie
  Hall (1960)
Day of the Gun (1962)
Reckless Men (1962)
The Moonlight War
  (1963)
Hogan's Way (1963)
The Dangerous Days of
  Kiowa Jones (1963)
Doomsday Creek (1964)
The Hottest Fourth of July
  in the History of
  Hangtree County (1964)
The Grabhorn Bounty
  (1965)
Shorty (1966)
A Partnership With Death
  (1967)
The Most Dangerous
  Profession (1967)
Dude Sheriff (1969)
Tragg's Choice (1969)
The Last Days of Wolf
  Garnett (1970)

Biscuit-Shooter (1971)
Rogue Cowboy (1971)
The Badge and Harry
  Cole (1972; as Lawman's
  Badge, UK, 1973)
Concannon (1972)
Hard Times and Arnie
  Smith (1972)
Once an Outlaw (1973)
The Hard Time Bunch
  (1973)
Hassle and the Medicine
  Man (1973)

As by Matt Kinkaid
Hardcase (1953)
The Race of Giants (1956)

As by Clay Randall
Six-Gun Boss (1952)
When Oil Ran Red (1953)
Boomer (1957)
The Oceola Kid (1963)
Hardcase for Hire (1963)

Amos Flagg—Lawman
  (1964)*
Amos Flagg—High Gun
  (1965)*
Amos Flagg Rides Out
  (1967)*
Amos Flagg—Bushwacked
  (1967)*
Amos Flagg Has His Day
  (1968; reprinted as The
  Killing of Billy
  Jowett,1973)*
Amos Flagg—Showdown
  (1969)*

Amos Flagg series

Black Gat Books

Black Gat Books is a new line of mass market paperbacks introduced in 2015 by Stark House Press. New titles appear every three months, featuring the best in crime fiction reprints. Each book is sized to 4.25" x 7", just like they used to be. Collect them all!

1 Haven for the Damned by Harry Whittington
978-1-933586-75-5, $9.99

2 Eddie's World by Charlie Stella
978-1-933586-76-2, $9.99

3 Stranger at Home by Leigh Brackett writing as George Sanders
978-1-933586-78-6, $9.99

4 The Persian Cat by John Flagg
978-1933586-90-8, $9.99

5 Only the Wicked by Gary Phillips
978-1-933586-93-9, $9.99

6 Felony Tank by Malcolm Braly
978-1-933586-91-5, $9.99

7 The Girl on the Bestseller List by Vin Packer
978-1-933586-98-4, $9.99

8 She Got What She Wanted by Orrie Hitt
978-1-944520-04-5, $9.99

9 The Woman on the Roof by Helen Nielsen
978-1-944520-13-7, $9.99

10 Angel's Flight by Lou Cameron
978-1-944520-18-2, $9.99

11 The Affair of Lady Westcott's Lost Ruby / The Case of the Unseen Assassin by Gary Lovisi
978-1-944520-22-9, $9.99

12 The Last Notch by Arnold Hano
978-1-944520-31-1, $9.99

Stark House Press

1315 H Street, Eureka, CA 95501 707-498-3135
griffinskye3@sbcglobal.net www.starkhousepress.com

Available from your local bookstore or direct from the publisher.